13

Fm
B   Barnard, Robert
        Too many notes, Mr.
        Mozart

TOO MANY NOTES,
MR. MOZART

TOO MANY NOTES, MR. MOZART

Robert Barnard

writing as

Bernard Bastable

Carroll & Graf Publishers, Inc.
New York

Originally published in Great Britain by Little, Brown and Co. in 1995

First Carroll & Graf edition 1996

Carroll & Graf Publishers, Inc.
260 Fifth Avenue
New York, NY 10001

ISBN 0-7867-0315-6

Library of Congress Cataloging-in-Publication Data is available.

Manufactured in the United States of America

AUTHOR'S NOTE

Most of the characters in this novel were historical personages. Many of them, however, have little more than a shadowy existence in diaries and memoirs of the period, and where this is the case I have felt at liberty to endow them with personalities that suited my story.

When the book was two or three chapters in, Claire Tomalin published her superb *Mrs Jordan's Profession*, a life of the mother of the FitzClarences. Though treating a much earlier period, it proved a treasure-trove of suggestions, and from her book I got, among much else, the climactic demand at the end of Chapter Six.

TOO MANY NOTES,
MR. MOZART

ONE
The New Pupil

The footman who admitted me to the palace apartment had a bedraggled look about him: his wig was askew and unpowdered, and his braid was parting company with his shoulder pads. When I had a moment to look around me I saw that the apartment itself was in a similar condition: its gilt was peeling, its paintwork was covered with a film of dirt, and the stuffing emerged shyly from several of its chairs. Kensington Palace was hardly the height of royal luxury, but this must be one of its dingier parts. It was clear that the King had other things to spend his money on than the living quarters of his widowed sister-in-law. Well, we all knew what the King preferred to spend his money on.

'Through 'ere, Mr Mozart,' said the footman, pronouncing my name in the detestable English fashion. He led the way down a long corridor with doors off it, until he came to a large, nearly empty room, quite as down-at-heel as the entry hall and corridor I had already passed through. There was a fortepiano over towards the window, and a few old chairs dotted around on a threadbare carpet. If this was the music room it did not suggest that music was a very important element in the life of this particular branch of the Royal Family.

'She'll be through in a minute,' said the footman. 'When they've finished their dinner.'

'My time is at the Princess's disposal,' I said, in a reproof at his familiarity with the Princess's name that totally failed to hit its target. The oaf nodded casually, grinned a street grin, and sauntered out of the chamber.

I looked around me. There was nothing in the room to lighten the burden of a long wait – no pictures worth more than a glance, no copies of *Bell's London Life* or *Jerry and Tom*. My time may have been at the Princess's disposal, but I didn't see why I should be bored to death. I went towards the fortepiano with great suspicion and played a few notes. It was an inferior instrument, just about in tune. Still, it was playable. I sat down and went through the second movement of a new sonata I was composing for Mr Novello (and probably for no one much else). It is a work for the much greater range and subtlety of the pianoforte but even on this instrument it made its effect. I had been playing for about five minutes when I heard the door opening. I stood up hurriedly and turned to the door.

The first figure to be ushered through by the tatty footman was a tiny sprite of a child, the second a heavy-featured, kindly-looking woman of a certain age (and well into it). I bowed low to them both, and the Princess came over and gave me a plump little hand, like a large soft doll's.

'Good afternoon, Mr Mozart. I am sorry you have had to wait. I am to be your new pupil – and a very poor one too, I daresay.'

She was wearing a drab grey dress – clean enough, but much washed, and her satin shoes looked similarly over-worn. Her face was not pretty or distinguished, being too pudgy for either quality, but she held herself with confidence and her protruberant eyes were notable not for Hanoverian dullness but for lightness and sparkle – they reminded me of bright marbles, or diamonds in a dirty corner. All in all the Princess had something her family had never been notable for: charm.

'I am honoured to be Your Royal Highness's new music teacher,' I said, kissing the hand.

'Your Royal Highness vill be a good pupil if you practise hard,' said the lady-in-waiting, in heavily accented English.

'Ah, there you are, you see,' said the sprite. 'Scales and arpeggios and things – terribly tedious. And if I *were* to practise hard, after ten minutes Sir John or somebody would come in and tell me I was driving them to distraction.'

The Princess pulled herself up on to the music stool – much too high for a tiny body like her – and played a few notes.

'But I intend to try my very, very hardest.' She turned to the lady-in-waiting. 'Do go and sit down, Späth, and Mr Mozart will find me something easy and pleasing to play.'

2

I bowed and sat down beside her.

'These days, Your Royal Highness, everyone seems to think Clementi is suitable for beginners,' I said, drawing some music from my bag and putting it on the stand in front of her. She looked at it, and her big eyes were widened theatrically.

'Too many notes, Mr Mozart!' she shrieked.

'But not at all as difficult as it looks,' I said. 'Clementi did not have the imagination to be difficult.'

'You will see!' she countered, launching into the first movement and pounding the keys with her sausagy fingers. Her enthusiasm was greater than her accuracy – much greater. In fact wrong notes positively flew around. 'You see?' she demanded, turning to me with a delightful smile. 'Far too many notes. What about something slow and pretty – something by yourself, perhaps, Mr Mozart?'

'Ah . . .' I said, hesitating. She was very quick and took me up at once.

'I see. You don't like beginners mangling your own music.'

'Not music that I prize,' I admitted.

'But *please*, Mr Mozart. So that when I am grown up I shall have one piece, one little piece, that I can say I play as *you* taught me to play it.'

It is sometimes said, by my children and others, that I am susceptible to flattery. Certainly I am very soft where young people are concerned. I took out the slow movement of one of my early sonatas and put it on the stand.

'Oh, much, much better,' she said, studying it for a moment. When she launched into it I could hear that there was definitely a modicum of musicianship in her playing, though she had not been well taught. I let her go on with it without interruption or correction, but when she had played about half a page of it I was astonished to hear the whispered words: 'She'll go to sleep in a minute or so.'

I looked at the Princess, hardly able to believe my ears. Her rosebud mouth was smiling slightly. I looked at the lady-in-waiting. She was sitting in a chair near the door, and she was indeed beginning to nod.

'Späth loves music – it always sends her to sleep,' whispered the Princess Victoria. 'Especially if she has had wine at dinner.

I pressed her to take a second glass.' She played on for a little longer. 'Is she off?' she asked.

'She does indeed seem to be asleep, Your Royal Highness,' I said. 'Soothed, perhaps, by your playing.'

She giggled.

'Perhaps you should play it for me, to show how it really goes.'

'I think you should –' I was about to say 'struggle through', but amended that to – 'make your own attempt at it first.'

'It's just that it must be so terribly painful for *you*,' she said kindly, performing a scale run of exquisite inaccuracy. 'Have you ever played before royalty before?'

'Many times, Your Royal Highness,' I said, surveying in my mind's eye the whole unhappy history. 'I performed at Windsor Castle when His present Majesty was just a young boy.'

She almost stopped playing in her astonishment.

'When Uncle King was a boy? But you must be shockingly old, Mr Mozart!'

'Shockingly,' I agreed. 'Though I was also quite young at the time.'

'And yet you have such a fine figure, and hardly look old at all,' she said. 'And Uncle King ... One day I was in Windsor Great Park, when I was *quite* young this was, and he went past in his carriage with Aunt May and ... a lady, and he stopped and took me up into his carriage and we went for such an exciting ride, with such wonderful horses drawing us, and such a tall footman behind. But there was little tiny me, much tinier then, up on the seat next to Uncle King with his e*nor*mous ...' she stopped short, obviously about to stop playing to illustrate the enormous stomach of her uncle, King George IV. 'Lehzen says I mustn't say anything disrespectful about Uncle King. So I won't.'

She played on a bit, but her mischievous expression clouded over after a moment or two. I soon learnt the reason why.

'I wouldn't say anything disrespectful about Uncle King in any case,' she said in serious tones, 'because everyone says he is very sick and like to die.'

'I believe His Majesty has been in poor health for some time,' I murmured.

4

'Do you know the expression "like to die"?' she demanded.

'It has quite a poetic ring to it,' I said.

'It's Shakespeare, or someone like that.'

'I'm glad you read Shakespeare,' I said. 'I have written an opera—'

'Oh yes, I love Shakespeare,' she enthused, her little pug face lighting up. 'There is an actor, Mr Braughton, comes to teach me el – elocution. Or he *used* to be an actor, or *wanted* to be an actor. I think he comes quite cheap. Sometimes I read the great speeches in Shakespeare, which is nice, though I don't imagine anyone will want me to read Shakespeare aloud to people when I'm grown up, do you? But sometimes we do scenes together, which is very exciting. Last week we did Hamlet and his mother, with him as Hamlet and me as his mother. Mr Braughton's copy of the play had a lot of stuff in it that wasn't in mine. It was very interesting, though I didn't understand it all.'

She took a deep breath. It had been a long speech, and I somehow got the idea it had been premeditated, though I couldn't for a moment imagine why it should have been. She was coming to the end of the sonata's slow movement.

'There!' she said. 'I got through it, though you couldn't say I did more than that.'

'It was a very creditable first attempt,' I said.

'Now you show me how it should go,' she insisted, climbing down from her stool. 'You will play it so beautifully that Späth will sleep on, and we can talk.'

I was beginning to wonder about the purpose of these piano lessons. I had the impression that the Princess had bottled up inside her a whole host of subjects which she was dying to talk about. So here was I, an elderly and neglected composer, *confidant* to the Hope of the Nation. Because that was what she was. Not many years before her birth the nation had faced the prospect of the throne going, one after the other, to a series of horrible and disreputable princes, none of them with legitimate heirs, followed by a series of princesses not much better. Now there were one or two legitimate heirs to these unsavoury scions of the royal house, but it was little Victoria who saved the nation from the dreadful possibility of her uncle the Duke of Cumberland being King. I could not but be delighted at the thought of being her friend. As I sat down and began, very softly and poetically, to play the same movement, she said, 'When Uncle Clarence becomes King, Mama says she will not let me go to court because I would meet the King's natural children. Are not all children natural, Mr Mozart?'

'Well, in a manner of speaking. But some children are . . . more natural than others.'

'Are your children natural, Mr Mozart?'

'No, no, my dear, my children are . . . Oh, I should not have said "My dear".'

'No, you should not. But I'm very glad you did . . . I was just teasing you about natural children, Mr Mozart.' The part of my mind that was not coping with her disconcerting conversation had been enjoying playing my own early music. Now I turned to look at her, and her face was wreathed in mischief. 'I know all about natural children,' she said. 'I should, shouldn't I? There seem to be more natural children than the other kind in my family.'

'We must not judge,' I said sententiously. 'There are many pressures on princes of the royal blood.'

'And not just princes,' she countered. 'But I wasn't judging anyway. It's just that natural children can't succeed to the throne, or titles, or anything like that. *So* . . .' She shot a glance in the direction of the sleeping Späth, whose mouth was open unprettily. 'So, when Uncle Clarence succeeds to the throne, I shall be next in line. Heiress Presumptive, that's what I shall be called. They think I don't know, but I do. I'm thinking of what to say when they tell me.'

'What to say?' I asked, startled yet again.

'Something memorable. For the History Books.'

I suppressed a smile.

'I see. Are you worried about the history books?'

'Not particularly, but I should like to be in them. At the moment nobody knows anything at all about me.'

'But they are interested. I should think that will all change when the Duke of Clarence becomes King.'

'Perhaps. But not if Mama has anything to do with it. She says I must be kept away from the corruption of the court. It's nothing to do with Uncle Clarence's natural children. She keeps me away from Uncle King's court, and she would even if he pressed her to bring me, which he doesn't. Have you ever been corrupted by the court, Mr Mozart?'

I had a feeling she was playing with me again, so I just looked down at her with a whimsical expression on my face.

'I have never really had the opportunity, Your Royal Highness.'

'Just like me! I thought you might have *sensed* it, at least . . . I think I should be allowed to go to court, so that I could see what terrible things I should avoid.'

At this wistful point in the conversation, my second movement came to an end, and I stood up.

'Oh, do please go on, Mr Mozart! Play something soft and peaceful then Späth will sleep on and on!'

'I think that would be unwise, Your Royal Highness. Anybody listening outside the door might realise it was not you playing.'

She giggled.

'They certainly would. You are quite right, Mr Mozart. They might wonder what the lessons are *for*.'

'Play it again, and we'll see what you've learnt from listening to me.'

I said it satirically, but the odd thing was that she had learnt something. When she had hauled herself up on to the stool she began it again, and played it much better. Clearly, though she had been talking the whole way through my playing, and talking very cleverly for an eleven-year-old, she had been absorbing the music at the same time. Späth dozed on.

'Do you know my Uncle Clarence?' the sprite asked, half-way through the first page.

'A little, my— Your Royal Highness.'

'*My dear*, you should say. Would you say he was a healthy man, Mr Mozart?'

That was an easy one to answer.

'Remarkably healthy for his years, my dear. No doubt due to his years at sea.'

'Good for seven or eight years, would you say?'

'Oh, we must hope for that and more.'

'Of course we must. But seven or eight would do. I would

7

not like to be Queen and have a Regent ruling. That would be most unfortunate for the Country.'

She gave a definite capital letter to the Country she would one day rule.

'Your uncle the King's time as Regent was generally counted one of the most glorious periods of our recent history,' I said hypocritically, remembering with aversion all those Allied Sovereigns and gluttonous feasts.

'Ah, but Grandpapa was mad, and everyone knew he could never recover and reign again. Uncle was King in all but name. It would be most unsuitable to have a Regent when I was growing up and having my own ideas about things. Particularly if there was also a Power Behind the Throne.'

She played a horribly wrong note, and there was a snort and a cough from the chair by the door.

'No, like *this*, Your Royal Highness,' I said, and leant over to play the phrase.

'Pay attention to Herr Mozart,' came a voice from by the door. 'You hev been playing most beautifully till now.'

The Princess played on for a bit, her fat little fingers really trying to give a musical interpretation of my notes.

'Is she off?' she whispered, scarcely able to contain her impatience.

'Yes, I think so,' I whispered back. I added, almost conspiratorially, 'Her mouth is slowly dropping open.'

'A sure sign . . . Mr Mozart?'

'Your Royal Highness?'

'I've heard it said that you've been of service to the Royal Family before – that you're very good at discovering things, getting to the truth of things.'

I had given a start when she talked about service to the Royal Family. How had she found out about the terrible business at the Queen's Theatre? The truth about that was only known to one or two people. Then I relaxed. The business she was referring to must be the little matter I sorted out for the Duke of Cumberland, a story for which the world is not yet ready.

'Your Royal Highness is referring to— ?'

'Uncle Cumberland, and the way you fixed things for him.'

I gave a little cough of reproof.

'I should prefer to say that I saved the Duke from embarrassment in a certain rather unpleasant matter.'

'You certainly did! Uncle Cumberland should have you permanently with him. He seems to spend his life being involved in rather unpleasant matters.'

'I'm not sure that I would care to be permanently attached to the Duke of Cumberland,' I said. I could say that without hesitation. The Duke is one member of the Royal Family that absolutely everyone feels he can speak ill of.

'No, indeed!' said the Princess feelingly. '*How* he looks at me! I've only met him twice but he made me shiver from head to toe. And Mama too. I think that if you can fix things for Uncle Cumberland, you must be a very clever man indeed, Mr Mozart.'

'And was my ability to fix things the reason why you asked for me as your piano teacher?' I guessed at a hazard. She played on for some moments, thinking how best to answer.

'Not ex*actly*,' she replied at last, a cunning expression coming into her eyes. 'And I didn't *ask*. I pushed and pressured and did all sorts of things, because they said that fifteen guineas a lesson was outrageous.'

'I put a high price on my service so as to have as few pupils as possible,' I said. Fearing that I had been tactless, I added, 'Not every young person is as musical as you, my—'

'My dear. What a shocking liar you are, Mr Mozart. Why I really wanted you was not to *fix* anything, so much as to find out the truth. That's what people say you did in the matter involving Uncle Cumberland.'

'Something of the sort,' I admitted.

'That's what I want you to do for me,' she said, a little flush of excitement on her face.

'Oh?'

'*Please*, Mr Mozart: *find out the truth about Mama and Sir John Conroy!*'

TWO
The Fat Cat

A minute or two later the lesson ended, which was probably just as well. The down-at-heel footman came in and announced that the Princess was due to go to Baroness Lehzen 'For 'er 'istory.' I wondered whether the lesson had been strictly timed, so that I could not charge extra. I kissed the Princess's hand, bowed to the lady-in-waiting (who was probably of some minor German noble order – I have to admit that titles are as common as paunches in that glorious country) and left the room in the company of that insouciant footman.

'Sir John will see you before you go,' he said chattily. 'To 'and over the cash, if you're lucky.' He added, perhaps meaning it kindly, 'You should hinsist on getting it each time, if you're wise.'

My mind, however, was still in a turmoil which had nothing to do with receiving my wages. To be asked by a young girl to spy on her own mother! Should I not have immediately repudiated the suggestion? And even if, for the odious word 'spy', one were to substitute some formulation such as 'enquire into the conduct of', still normally the request would leave an unpleasant taste in the mouth. Why had I not spluttered my outrage, put her down with an 'Out of the question'?

Was it because she was a child, and I am susceptible to children? Was it because she was a princess and 'like to be' (as she might have put it) Queen before too long? Or was it because, in her approach to the subject, there was a basic seriousness, a sense of responsibility, a feeling that the power that Sir John Conroy might have in the event of her mother's Regency would be power that was against all the best interests of the country as a whole?

10

My disordered thoughts were terminated by the footman's knocking at a door in the long corridor and ushering me into a room. It was a largish sitting room, the furniture better than in the entrance hall, but not much – faded and old-fashioned, the sofa badly in need of re-covering. It was a woman's room, but the room of a woman without any particular skills at home-making. Perhaps home-making was impossible in a place like Kensington Palace. There was a desk over by one of the windows, and at it sat a man. I felt a twinge of something wrong, something inappropriate. I did not feel it right that the Duchess's Comptroller should sit even temporarily at a desk in her sitting room. It seemed to hint at a relationship between them that was closer, more permanent than that of employer and employee. Perhaps it was my old-fashioned sense of etiquette. Perhaps the Princess Victoria had aroused my suspicions.

'Ah, Mr Mozart,' the man said, coming over to me, his hand outstretched.

Sir John Conroy was a man of military bearing, well set up, only just beginning to be fleshy. Why then did I have the impression of a fat cat? His cheeks were plumped out, side-whiskered, and his dark eyes were penetrating. All in all he had the air of a man who was doing very well for himself – an air that contrasted oddly with the shabbiness of the surroundings. He also gave the impression that he was a man who thought very well of himself. One might also say he had an air of fatal over-confidence. I bowed to him.

'Sir John Conroy?'

'Yes. I am the Comptroller of Her Royal Highness's Household. I am delighted to make your acquaintance, Mr Mozart. The lesson went well?'

'It went extremely well,' I said, gilding the lily a bit, as one does when royalty is in question. 'There are one or two bad habits that the Princess has acquired from her previous teacher, but once those have been eradicated—'

'We can have great hopes for the future, can we?' he said, interrupting with a military man's geniality. 'Good, good. You feel that the Princess is musical then, do you? Would repay your efforts?'

'Certainly I do.' Was I, I wondered, being sparing with the

truth? My son Charles Thomas, who has moved down from the north to teach at the West Hammersmith College for Young Ladies, and also, I suspect, to keep an eye on my welfare (why else would one move from a region of great musicality to teach the cloth-eared Londoners?), says that a child, particularly a girl, can twist me round her little finger. I *did* want to continue teaching the young Victoria – quite apart from the incidental benefits of a royal position – prestige, incidental employment, *credit.* Nevertheless I *did* sense in the Princess the seeds of a fresh, delightful musicality. Mind you, the present King is musical, in a way. He likes Rossini. A genuinely musical sovereign would be a great boon to the country.

'I suppose you have to convince yourself your pupils are musical,' said Sir John, with a surface, man-of-the-world geniality that did nothing to disguise the tactlessness of the remark. 'Now, about your fee—'

I took an instant decision.

'Ah yes, the fee,' I said. He looked up at me suspiciously. He thought I was going to raise it, and was preparing to fight. 'I always in preliminary discussions set the fee on the high side, to discourage run-of-the-mill pupils. When I have a pupil of genuine musical promise, I set the fee at a more . . . realistic level.'

'Really?' Sir John suddenly exuded good humour.

'The Princess is, I believe, musical by nature, with a good ear. There is also the natural interest of her position. She could in the future do much for British music. I suggest we set the fee at seven guineas.'

'Done, Mr Mozart!'

Sir John was clearly a man to whom a few guineas mattered. So, for that matter, was I, but I was conscious of the many advantages involved in being the Princess Victoria's music master. Sir John rubbed his hands.

'You will not regret this, Mr Mozart. The Princess must have inherited her musical ear from her mother. The Duchess as you know is German, and you Germans are always musical, are you not? If the Princess should inherit the throne in the near future – we will, of course, hope that is not her fate! – English music could expect much patronage from the Duchess when she is Queen Mother and Regent.'

12

I was flabbergasted at the ignorance of the man. How could the Duchess of Kent be Queen Mother when she had never been Queen? It was not a title, in any case, that the British set great store by. Their kings tended to outlive their consorts as a rule. The last person to use the title, if my memory served, was Queen Henrietta Maria after the Restoration. And her widowhood came on her prematurely, so to speak.

My astonishment must have got into my face, because Sir John said, 'The title could be bestowed by Parliament, in gratitude to the Duchess for her upbringing of their Queen. We are in the hands of Parliament in this country, are we not?'

I had misjudged the man. Slightly. He was not ignorant, merely naive. I bowed, not wishing to waste any words on the unlikely concept of a grateful Parliament. Sir John sensed he had been unwise and hastened to change the subject.

'Should we be shortly at the beginning of a new reign, the Duchess would wish the Princess to be better known to the country at large.'

'Naturally,' I said. 'Though difficult to accomplish, with the Princess so young.'

'What I – what the Duchess has in mind is journeys around the country, to make the Princess acquainted with her future kingdom and its people.'

That sounded like a pleasant break from the gloomy monotony of Kensington Palace.

'That would certainly be educational and enjoyable for her,' I said cautiously. 'Though I suppose there would be the susceptibilities of the new King and Queen to consider.'

With a brisk wave of his strong right hand Sir John dismissed the susceptibilities of the new King and Queen.

'On these tours – progresses, we might call them – the Princess would naturally stay at the First Houses of the neighbourhoods she was visiting. We would wish the Princess, when she mixes for the first time with the country's nobility and gentry, to be a credit to her upbringing and education.'

'I have no doubt that she will be,' I said, sincerely but mystified.

'Quite,' said Sir John heartily. 'We would hope that among

other things, she would be able to acquit herself creditably on the pianoforte.'

Ah, that was it. I was to teach her pretty or brilliant pieces that would arouse facile applause in the homes of the nobs. Somehow I could not see the Princess taking tamely to the role of puppet performer. There was something subversive in her – not subversive of the general order of things, for she was very tenacious of her place in that, but subversive of her mother and Sir John's view of the order of things.

'As Her Royal Highness's musical education proceeds,' I said, with a touch of stiffness, 'she will naturally acquire pieces that she could play publicly, should she wish to.'

Sir John's strong right hand seemed about to indulge in another dismissive wave suggesting that Princess Victoria's wishes were neither here nor there, but he restrained it at the last minute. His impatience with the proprieties of his position vis-à-vis the Princess was interesting – it was as strong, in a different way, as the oafish footman's who now interrupted us by opening the door to permit the entrance of a large lady.

I had seen the Duchess of Kent before, but only once. She was not a lady who went much into Society, or was to be seen in public places. She was neither popular nor unpopular with the nation at large: she was simply unknown. It was said that she had made a good wife to the Duke of Kent during their brief marriage, perhaps because he was marginally less awful than her first husband. She was by birth a princess of Saxe-Coburg, a German Duchy so small and obscure that no royal family but the British would contemplate marrying into it. She had children by her first husband, so her child-bearing capacity was proven – perhaps that was the attraction. She was an ample woman, carefully but not well dressed, with an open manner, and with the remains of handsomeness still on her face. She seemed friendly, and she was more tactful than most of the members of the Royal Family I had met, but even on that first visit I conceived the idea that she was not a wise woman. By which I think I mean that she was a very poor judge of men and measures.

'Ah, you must be Mr Mozart,' she said, coming straight over. 'Späth tells me you have already vorked miracles with

14

the Princess's playing.' I bowed low and kissed her hand. 'Ve are compatriots, are ve not, Mr Mozart, or more or less? But ve must talk English for Sir John's sake. Sir John has been my faithful Comptroller for many years now, but I have never tried to teach him German. I'm sure you understand vy. It is most important that the Princess hears only English around her. The public at large is so prejudiced against anything German!'

She seemed to be giving me a great deal of information and opinion on a first acquaintanceship. Sir John interrupted her flow.

'Mr Mozart and I have come to a most satisfactory agreement on the matter of Her Royal Highness's lessons,' he said.

'Ah!' she said, understanding at once, and expressing her satisfaction. 'You see, Mr Mozart, ve are not rich. It is impossible to live in the sort of manner that the Princess's position demands on the money that Parliament has voted us. And then the King – but then, I do not complain. The poor King is very near his end. But as Her Royal Highness grows up, and as the time approaches ven her Destiny is almost on her – *then* the country vill understand that things must be done in a proper style. And then ve will be able to reward you as you deserve, Mr Mozart!'

At the age of seventy-three one ceases to look forward to honey tomorrow, and would much prefer honey today. However, I bowed my gratitude for favours unreceived. The Duchess hardly noticed in the fullness of her flow.

'The Princess Victoria, whom of course I dearly love—'

Mothers who say that of course they dearly love their children are always about to expatiate on their failings. I steeled myself. I already knew whose side I was on.

'—is inclined to be headstrong, inclined to vant her own vay. You must try to curb that, Mr Mozart. It runs in the family, and it has brought misery to the country and dishonour to the royal house. My aim is to bring up my daughter as simply and as naturally as possible, and to keep her far removed from corrupting influences. I intend to see that my daughter, ven she is Queen, is viewed by the country as a *fresh start.*'

'Her youth will ensure that, ma'am,' I pointed out. 'In the course of nature she will still have that when she ascends the throne.' For the sake of the little sprite I added, 'On the other hand she must know how to take her place as Sovereign.'

'She vill know her *duties*, Mr Mozart, and she vill do them,' said the Duchess, with a touch of reproof in her voice. 'As regards the circle who vill surround her, I myself, sadly used as I am to courts, vill be better able to deal with them. She vill have a very different court to any ve have known in this country. It has fortunately been no problem to keep her away from the present court. His Majesty has shown no vish to know his brother's child. Perhaps he has some idea of the unsuitability of those who, alas, surround him. Ven the Duke of Clarence succeeds, things may become much more difficult.'

'The Duke is a genial man,' I ventured.

'Very genial, and already inclined to make advances.'

'It would be sad if there were . . . ruptures, if the advances were not reciprocated.'

I had gone too far.

'Have you *heard* the Duke's style of conversation, Mr Mozart?'

'Somewhat salty, I believe, Your Royal Highness.'

'Scandalously free! He simply cannot control himself. And to think of my innocent child at court, surrounded by FitzClarences, by his b——. But it doesn't bear thinking about. Sad it may be to keep my child from any such advances, but it is also inevitable.'

I bowed a reluctant agreement. Sir John obviously decided that this conversation had gone on long enough. He did not like listening to other people's opinions. He began scrabbling in a cash box, and emerged with seven golden guineas. He was about to hand them over, rather as he might have paid his coal merchant, when the door opened.

'Vicky! What a priceless lad your footman is. Oh hello, John. When he opened the door to me he said "Will you go on in, or shall I hannounce you?" Wonderful!'

'He is proving hard to train,' admitted Sir John.

'Don't try! Retain him in his natural state. The only savage royal footman in captivity. And *this* must be Mr Mozart.'

She had now joined the little group by the desk, moving a little uncertainly, like someone with poor eyesight who declines to wear glasses. She was a woman in her fifties, but both her face and her manner retained a gracefulness and charm that warmed the heart. She was better dressed than the Duchess, though not richly or fashionably: she showed what could be done on a limited income, and refrained from the foolish habit some older women have of bedecking themselves in too much jewellery, which only draws attention to the fact that the jewellery is the only thing about them that is fine. She seemed altogether a warmer, truer person than the Duchess, and if there was a touch of silliness there, it was an essential part of her charm.

'The Princess Sophia – Mr Mozart,' murmured Sir John.

'The reason I am here, *of course*,' said the Princess, fixing me with a captivating smile. 'Forgive me if I come close: I can't make you out otherwise. I had to come over from *my* little set of boxes to pay homage. What *pleasure* you gave us all in my young days, Mr Mozart! You are too young to remember, John, and you, Vicky. But your *Figaro*, and above all your wonderful *Don Giovanni*! How well I remember the handsomeness of the Don himself – all London was in love with him. How we thrilled to the sound of his voice, how we cried for him when he was taken off to hell. Oh dear, such times they were, such wonderful times in the theatre! We shan't see their like again.'

'I have written another opera—' I began.

'And *Così Fan Tutte* – why did nobody like it so much? The music was divine – a heavenly feast! And it was so wise and witty about men, and women, and love.'

How she wormed her way into my heart with that judgement!

'Your Royal Highness is among the very select and distinguished few who appreciate the work,' I murmured.

'Caviare to the general!' she agreed. 'But what wonderful popular successes the others were! Anyone can have a popular success of the Rossini sort, but a popular success with an opera like *Figaro* – it was an act of public education. You must introduce little Victoria to the opera: let her play the main airs, then make sure she is taken there.'

'There is, I believe, an opera by Rossini in preparation at Covent Garden,' I said sourly. 'The Cinderella subject. It could be suitable, if they don't mess around with it.'

'They will. What a pity my brother is dying. He could have taken her.' The expression on the Duchess's face said 'over my dead body', but the Princess could not see her, and had turned to Sir John. 'When my poor brother dies, John, I shall need entire new mourning.'

'But Your Royal Highness had—'

'I had new mourning when Fred died, and that's three years ago, and has done for four foreign royalties since. George is not just a brother, he is the *King*. So you'll just have to stump up. And I am very fond of Georgie. All of us girls are. He understood us, and tried to help us. He realised we had needs, and couldn't forever sit posed in a family group around Mama.' She turned to me. 'Papa loved us and thought nothing about us. One wouldn't have thought that possible, but that's the truth of it.'

I wasn't quite sure how to deal with the personal confidences of a princess.

'His Majesty no doubt had much to exercise his mind,' I said tactfully.

'Oh, I loved Papa, and would never abuse him. Especially not to you, Mr Mozart. He was your great benefactor, was he not?'

Those fifty guineas! Those damned fifty guineas! Given to my poor father after a recital the like of which a seven-year-old had never before performed – and given, I am quite certain, because the King's flunkey misheard 'fifteen' for 'fifty'. They were the cause of my father's fatal decision to stay in this fog-bound bog of insularity, instead of returning to wonderful, artistic, intellectual Austria, our homeland, country of my heart – country where my genius would have been appreciated, instead of constantly slighted!

I was still swallowing down my emotion when Sir John at last handed over the shining seven guineas and began ushering me towards the door.

'We must not keep you any longer, Mr Mozart. Your girls will be awaiting you.'

'My – my girls?' I said in shocked surprise. What lies had people told him about my private life?

'Your young ladies at Hammersmith. But I suppose you are finished teaching there for the day.'

18

Outside the cheery oaf of a footman escorted me to the door of the apartment.

'See you next week,' he said. 'Mind what I said about the dibs. If you don't get it on the spot, you never will.'

I made no reply to him, because I was still digesting the last words of Sir John Conroy. So they had engaged me in mistake for my son, had they? No wonder they had jibbed at the fee. Though wait: they had expressed no surprise at Princess Sophia's remarks about my operas. Probably they had managed to coalesce in their minds – which were not, assuredly, artistic minds – the two of us into one, and had thought that the composer of *Don Giovanni* had sunk in his last years to being music teacher at a girls' school. Well, let me not denigrate my own son! It would be no worse than being the largely forgotten, neglected, unperformed composer I have actually sunk to being, with no friend except the good Mr Novello.

I walked home – not bad at seventy-three! – sunk in thought. I really needed to take stock of the position I had suddenly got myself into. I was now committed to investigating the relationship between the Duchess of Kent and Sir John Conroy, and I was doing it at the instigation of her daughter, the Princess Victoria. I had not said I agreed to her suggestion, but I had not repudiated it indignantly. I knew I was going to do it, and she, the little minx, knew I was going to as well. And if I asked myself *why*, I could only say that I liked the Princess and felt sorry for her.

And because I rather liked investigating things.

That said, the *how* presented problems that might prove insuperable, and might mean I had to disappoint my little pupil entirely. My visits to the palace would be brief and entirely professional. How could I use them to investigate whether Sir John and the Duchess shared 'the rank sweat of an enseaméd bed' (which the Princess doubtless heard about from the uncommonly full text of *Hamlet* that Mr Braughton had regaled her with, and which had possibly put the idea of her mother's relationship with Sir John into her sharp little head)?

But as I thought about the difficulties of the investigation a possibility, an avenue of approach, suggested itself. Perhaps the chatty ruffian of a footman could be useful.

I thought, next, about the little princess and her situation. She had made me feel right from the start that I stood almost *in loco parentis* towards her – an odd relationship for a music teacher to a royal pupil! Probably this was partly her cunning, but probably it was partly due to her feelings of inadequacy, or worse, of her real parent. I considered the people whom I had met at the palace: the Princess Sophia, charming, artistic, a little silly; the Duchess, serious, intense, yet somehow unwise; and then Sir John Conroy . . .

It was clear that Sir John, if he aimed to stand *in loco parentis* to the future Queen, was going the wrong way about it. He came very near to implying to me that her wishes and preferences were of no account at all. A domineering but not a sensible man, then, though a superficially attractive one. He could certainly gain an influence over a grown woman, if not young girls. The Princess Sophia had called him 'John', though the Duchess had been more cautious and more formal.

Was he the lover of one, or both, of them? That was what I was bidden to find out. But another question had occurred to me while still in his company. The Duchess lived a frugal life, in tatty surroundings. I was willing to bet the Princess Sophia's circumstances were hardly more luxurious. Yet Parliament had voted a sum – perhaps not a generous but yet a substantial one, for the upkeep of the Duchess and her daughter, and for George III's daughter. Could that sum really not buy a style of living better than this? If Sir John was pleasuring them, was he also swindling them?

This thought lasted me till I sank down to a substantial meal in Mr Benbow's Chop House in the Strand. My account with Mr Benbow had quite recently been settled up (by Mr Novello, it must be said, rather than by any impulsive action of my own), and so he was unusually polite. He was fascinated by my acquaintance with the unknown Princess in Kensington Palace, and pressed me for details – he was himself a father of girls, and considered himself an expert. His interest was increased by the fact (which he said he had heard on the Highest Authority) that the King was sinking. I took no notice. The King had been sinking for so long

20

that even sensible people believed he would go on sinking for ever.

Next morning I was awoken by my maid Susan with the news that he had finally sunk.

THREE
Majesty

The British people were unusually uninhibited in their expressions of delight at the death of the King. They put off their habitual hypocrisy and were honest in their emotions for once. They had never liked or trusted him. He had given them circuses when what they needed was bread, and in his last years he had retreated into melancholia and hypochondria, and had not even put on any kind of show. The British people were tired of paying his enormous debts, tired of a monarch who was both reactionary and weak. They were yearning for a king who was more accessible, more visible, and above all cheaper.

Which was precisely what they got. If the King's heir had been the Duke of Cumberland they might have summoned up some show of grief for the dead man out of hatred for his successor. But as it was the Duke of Clarence, all they could express was joy at the change. Even his successor hardly bothered to feign sorrow, and the funeral was a jolly, chatty affair, with the enormous coffin largely disregarded. By the time he had been King for a few days William IV was pottering around his capital, greeting and shaking hands with everyone, being kissed by a whore in St James's, and generally behaving like an amiable grocer who wants to keep in with his customers.

I received a note from Kensington Palace intimating that the death of the King should not alter arrangements for the Princess's music lessons. It did not surprise or shock me: if the new King did not pretend grief, why should his sister-in-law? I gave the Princess her second lesson, and the Baroness Späth again demonstrated her musicality by dropping off.

'Have you thought about what I asked you to do, Mr Mozart?'

asked the Princess in a conspiratorial murmur.

'Very much,' I replied. 'Against my better judgement I have decided to do what I can to help Your Royal Highness—'

'It is *not* against your better judgement at all!' protested the Princess Victoria, with an obstinate tilt to her chin. 'It's the best judgement you could make.'

'—provided, I was about to say, you practise like a demon and play for me like an angel.'

She had no problem detecting the twinkle in my eye.

'Oh, I'll try!' she said, playing with exaggerated expressiveness. 'But I expect I'll practise like an angel and play for you like a demon.'

That was about all we said that was germane to the matter, and I was unable to pursue at that visit the avenue of enquiry I had decided on because the scruffy footman was off-duty on the day of the lesson.

On the day succeeding my plans were further altered, and in a surprising way. I received a note from Lord Egremere, telling me that the new King and his family, having removed themselves with remarkable speed to Windsor, were holding an intimate party for family and friends the following Saturday to which he was invited. The Queen was most anxious, Lord Egremere said, that I should be one of the guests, and should give a short recital.

If he'd said the King wanted me to play I wouldn't have believed him. Hornpipes on a penny whistle were about the extent of his musical cultivation by all accounts. The Queen, however, was an unknown quantity, and everyone was disposed to think well of her in their general pleasure at having a queen again, and a respectable one at that. It did surprise me that I had an unknown admirer among the Royal Family that I had hitherto known nothing of. Where royalty is concerned these things tend to get around. If I had known that she admired my music I would have used the information in the only sensible way possible – to gain credit. Still, I swallowed my doubts and agreed to play.

Lord Egremere has aged. Of course I have aged too, and in many ways my life has slowed down and simplified itself. I seldom lead the orchestra at the Queen's Theatre or anywhere else, though I still give recitals when I am asked. Lord Egremere, however, walks with great difficulty, using two sticks, frequently grimacing with pain. When I contrast this with my own mobility I give thanks for my frugal way of life (enforced by my frugal finances), and my chaste habits.

Lord Egremere, the moment I got into his coach, showed he was enormously puffed up and excited by the King's invitation.

'It means that he wants to hold out the hand of friendship to the Whigs,' he said, signalling to the coachman to continue on our way. 'He wants to be King to the whole nation.'

I did not remind him that similar things were said of the late King at the time of his accession. The hopes had been as evanescent as winter sunshine. But Lord Egremere positively bounced with optimism, and I could only hope it was justified. The country had had term after term of Tory rule, sinking further and further into scruffiness and lawlessness. Most men of goodwill felt there must be hope for the Whigs and Reform at last.

'We must hope that the royal goodwill is lasting,' I said cautiously.

'Oh, it will be, it will be. Say what you like about the new King, he is straight. Doesn't have the brains to dissimulate. And he was very sound on the Catholic Question. Oh no, he won't be a bar to reform.'

As the coach sped on towards Windsor I fervently hoped he was right, and made no further attempts to dampen the poor old chap's high spirits.

The new King's jollity and democratic ways had not yet effected any change in the stiff formality of Windsor Castle and its staff. However, as soon as the posse of functionaries had led us to the Green Drawing Room we could see the royal geniality at close quarters, and we had to agree that it made an immense difference to the atmosphere of court life. Though everyone was naturally wearing mourning, there was a buzz of talk and laughter, and everything was more relaxed than I would have conceived possible. At the centre of things was the King himself – plump, red, with his pineapple head bobbing excitedly, going round to everyone, shaking hands, kissing the pretty women, exchanging platitudes, opinions, jokes and gossip. He darted here and there with no idea of formality or precedence, and when he spotted Lord Egremere he charged over as if they were the oldest friends in the world, though I was convinced they barely knew each other.

'And this is Mr Mozart, is it?' he said, when they had exchanged greetings, turning in my direction. His voice was far from mellifluous, but one warmed to geniality. I bent over his hand. 'Pooh – don't bother with that. Shake hands like a man. Saw one of your pieces once. *The Jolly Tar*. Very tuneful and pretty. Not much like naval life, though.'

'I'm sure it was not, Your Majesty,' I said deprecatingly. 'I just write the music.'

'Of course – that's how it's done, isn't it? Another feller writes the words and you just set them to tunes. Used to know a lot about the theatre when . . . Pay you well for that, do they?' He roared with laughter when I shook my head. 'Nice tunes they were, anyway.'

'Your Majesty could do with some fine music for your coronation,' said Lord Egremere. The King went redder and spluttered.

'Coronation? Who says I have to be crowned? A lot of mummery. If they insist on it I'll write a note to the Archbishop saying it'll be the day after next, and then I'll walk down to the Abbey and he can clap the crown on my head and that'll be that. There'll be none of the damned medieval nonsense there was last time. Sacrilegious, if you ask me. If they want music you can write 'em a hymn tune, eh, Mr Mozart? Any good at hymn tunes?'

'I haven't often been called upon for them,' I admitted.

'Can't be difficult. Simple words, simple metres. "God Save the King" can't have taken much writing, can it?'

'The Queen may want a more elaborate coronation than you have in mind, sir,' said Lord Egremere.

'Humph! Adelaide's a good woman. She does what she's told. Ah – Lord Grey! . . .'

And he dashed off, duty done, to chat away in a high-speed rattle to the prominent Whig peer whose star was in the ascendant.

'The Dutch had William the Silent. We seem to have William the Never Silent,' I murmured to Lord Egremere.

25

Now that the King had moved on we had time to look about us. King William, jogging around from person to person, naturally made one centre of the glittering assembly. The other, still centre was the new Queen. She sat calmly in one of the splendidly uncomfortable chairs, looking as if she would like to have a piece of embroidery with her, so as to have something to do with her hands. Her mourning dress was a fine black silk, with no style about it at all. She was a plain, gentle, conventional-looking woman, sliding into middle-age, anxious to do the right thing, and to be liked. I had no doubt she did what she was told. My Connie would have thought that a poor epitaph, but times change ... Near to the Queen were her lady-in-waiting, one or two lords and ladies that I recognised, and a group of young people, notably good-looking and lively, who seemed to know the Queen much better than anyone else, and to behave quite freely in her presence.

'The FitzClarences,' murmured Lord Egremere. 'Their time has come, and they mean to make the most of it while it lasts.'

I looked at them with renewed interest: the King's bastard brood by Mrs Jordan, an actress I had not known well – she was one of Sheridan's company at Drury Lane – but one whom I admired enormously. Her children certainly had her good looks. At this point the Queen looked up, seemed to recognise me, and beckoned Lord Egremere over to introduce us.

'Ah, Mr Mozart,' she said, in clear, slightly painstaking English, as I was bowing. 'You will be so kind as to play for us later on?'

'I shall be happy to, Your Majesty,' I said.

'I am so fond of your music,' she said, but in a vague, almost an embarrassed way. I realised at once that she was lying, and didn't like lying.

'Is your music *very* old-fashioned?' asked one of the pretty young ladies around her.

'Elizabeth! How can you be so rude?'

'Oh, but Mama, Mr Mozart is not a young man, and does not pretend to be one, unlike the late King.'

'I am indeed very old, Lady Erroll,' I said, recognising the one FitzClarence I had seen before – one who had been very

26

much in Society since her marriage. 'And my music is indeed old-fashioned. But perhaps, as with furniture, good quality transcends fashion.'

'A very good answer!' said the Queen.

'But of course every new generation wants to like something different from their parents,' I went on.

'So sad, so silly,' sighed the Queen.

'Not at all, Mama Queen,' said a lowering, handsome man, who looked to be the eldest of the FitzClarences. 'Perfectly natural that what we like now is not what you liked in your youth. And that what you liked is not what my father liked in his youth.'

'Well, well,' said the Queen, rising and leading the way over to a superb grand piano. 'I think, George, we will ask Mr Mozart to play before anyone mentions Rossini. I am told that Rossini is not to be talked about in his presence.'

As the Queen approached the instrument the voices in the room fell silent one by one, until only the King's voice was to be heard, telling an embarrassing story about a lady who was probably in the room. Then that was stilled, the Queen inclined her head to me, and I sat down and began to play.

I knew better than to play anything grand or beautiful. I played instead a succession of encore pieces – dances, marches, ending in compliment to the King with an arrangement of a well-known hornpipe. The programme left me ample scope for reflection. My first thoughts centred on the Queen. She was on the surface a dowdy little thing, though perfectly nice and peace-loving, so far as I could judge. Her final remark about Rossini, which could have been humorous and sly, was apparently said in total seriousness. On the other hand she understood her new position, could enforce silence, ensure proper consideration for herself.

Except perhaps from the FitzClarences. Their attitude to her seemed ambiguous. On the one hand they stressed their relationship with 'Mama Queen', no doubt as a way of underlining their new status as the King's children. It was well known that the Duke of Clarence, when he took a wife, had insisted that it must be someone who was willing to be a mother to his brood of natural children. Adelaide had clearly taken the responsibility seriou..y, and all credit was due to her.

The children, on the other hand, seemed to mingle affection and contempt in their attitude to her. George had seemed to want to stress that she was of a different generation from her husband, and that he had had a life before he married her. That, perhaps, was natural: the FitzClarences were the product of that life, and they would all have vivid memories of their mother before her abandonment and death. Many of them, indeed, would have been grown up before Adelaide came into their lives.

I played for fifteen minutes. I couldn't risk more. Already ominous barking sounds were coming from the direction of the King's chair. As I took my bows and let the party resume its chattering and laughing, the King came over.

'Very nice, very nice. You've certainly got a way with a tune, Mr Mozart. Thought I recognised that last one.'

'It's a well-known hornpipe, Your Majesty.'

'Ah, that'd be it. Didn't know you'd wrote it. Needs a lot of midshipmen, clapping in time. Couldn't get this stuffy lot to do it.'

He looked around disparagingly.

'The court seems remarkably *un*stuffy and relaxed, sir,' I ventured. 'In comparison to—'

'To m'brother's court?' said His Majesty, with a complacent little smile. He had obviously been disparaged and kept in obscurity for so long that he relished praise. 'Well, we do our best. Can't expect things to change overnight, what? I suppose you think I'm unfeeling, do you?'

I was taken aback by the abruptness of the accusation.

'Your Majesty?'

'Unfeeling. Not to put on a great show of grief for poor old George. Lot of nonsense, mourning. I don't like shows. Pantomimes. George was never much of a brother to me. All he ever taught me was the price of a whore – down to the price of a quick go against a wall. Useful. But not what you'd call a liberal education.' All this had been said in quarterdeck tones, with the Queen no more than a few feet away. Now he lowered his voice, a thing he obviously found difficult. 'Mr Mozart – I wonder if I might have a few words with you?'

Ah! My doubts about the Queen's love of music were going to be justified.

'Of course, Your Majesty.'

Already he was leading the way across the Drawing Room, and once away from the press of courtiers he jogged through a little chapel, down the grandiose length of St George's Hall, past a staircase, then through other grand rooms, talking all the time about nothing very much. Finally we landed up at the other end of the State Apartments, in a small room, decorated in dark, claretty red, with something of the air of a study. Candles were already set there, and the footman who had followed us from the Drawing Room stood by the door and waited. The King nodded to him to fill my glass, then nodded to him to leave us alone. He had rather an eloquent nod.

'Take a seat, Mr Mozart. No ceremony here. Lot of stuff and nonsense, all that. We never had any, Adelaide and me, when we were at home at Bushey. M'brother George liked it, and could carry it off. He had an air. Not a lot of use, an air, if you ask me. Where were we?'

'Your Majesty wanted a word with me.'

'Oh yes, of course ... Hear you're giving piano lessons to m'neice.'

Ah, ha!

'I do have that honour, sir.'

'How does she strike you?'

I cleared my throat.

'I couldn't presume to—'

The King showed signs of impatience.

'Come along, man. None of this flim-flam. What sort of a gel is she?'

'Well, sir ... Rather bright. Sharp. Sees things, wants to get at the truth of things.'

He nodded, pleased.

'Quite right. She'll need to. Knowing little thing?'

'Something of the sort, sir. Honourable, straightforward. Very conscious of her position.'

He nodded his pineapple head.

'So she should be. Adelaide's never going to produce now. Poor woman – she feels it very much. We had a baby, you know, and it died. Still weeps for it. But Victoria's the heir, no doubt about that.'

'She is conscious of her position in line to the throne, sir, though those around her think she is not.'

The King roared with laughter.

'Cunning little thing! She's had to be, probably. We want to get to know her better.'

'I think you will find that she wants that very much herself.'

The King smiled in satisfaction.

'Always behaved very prettily when we've seen her. Which isn't often. Adelaide's always tried to be a good aunt to the gel. Mother's the problem.'

I tried to enter into the subject tactfully.

'Her mother seems to think that court would be a corrupting influence.'

The King went red.

'Stuff and nonsense! Courts are dull as ditchwater. She should know that . . . Funny woman. Good wife to Edward, while he lasted. Wasn't long. Maybe she was lucky. Funny chap too, Edward. All the girls in the family loved him, but he had a taste for flogging soldiers to death. Odd taste, that . . . You think the mother will stand in our way with the gel?'

'I think it's possible, Your Majesty.'

His extraordinary head bobbed up and down, as if it were on the water.

'Ye-e-es, that's what we think. We need something to put pressure on her. Tell you the truth, that's why I wanted a word with you, Mr Mozart.'

'With me, sir? I assure you I have no influence—'

He leaned forward in his chair.

'You're a sharp fellow. That's known in our circle. Fixed things for m'brother Ernest. Anyone who can get him out of a scrape must be a genius.'

He felt in the pocket of his coat, and his hand emerged with a large chamois leather bag. Without ceremony he handed it over. My practised hand knew at once that it contained a considerable number of guineas.

'Your Majesty! I am overwhelmed! I don't know anything that I can do that would earn—'

'Here's what you can do. Find out the truth about her mother and Sir John Conroy!'

FOUR

Lackey

'Well?' said the Princess Victoria.

She said it the moment the first gentle snore wafted over to us from the chair by the door, after five minutes of her third lesson with me.

'Play on, Your Royal Highness,' I said. 'It's too early to tell whether there has been any improvement yet.'

'Oh, bother improvement!' said the Princess, but she played on nevertheless. 'Actually, I have practised and practised for you, Mr Mozart. And do you know what the interesting thing is?'

'No.'

'I haven't improved one little bit. Isn't that strange?'

'Not really,' I said, being very used to that situation. 'There is practice where you try to eradicate your faults, and there is practice where you just repeat them over and over again. Yours must have been of the second kind.'

'I suppose it must . . . Eradicate. I suppose that means "get rid of". I must remember that. There are some people I should very much like to eradicate . . . Anyway, you know perfectly well, Mr Mozart, that I wasn't asking about my playing.'

'Yes.'

'Well?'

I tried to sound magisterial, full of wisdom born of long experience.

'Your Royal Highness must understand the nature of an investigation of this kind. It is not something that can be rushed. For a start, the information that is sought is of a peculiarly delicate kind. That means the sources of that imformation have to be subtly softened, cultivated, until they are willing to reveal what they know.'

The Princess looked impressed.

'How extremely fascinating! I should so like to be an investigator.' She thought for a moment. 'Of course, by rights I should be one of the sources you are talking about.'

'That would hardly be right—'

'I don't see why not.' She had a very obstinate streak when she was contradicted, and raised her chin, which truth to tell was almost non-existent. 'I think it would be perfectly natural. You see, I sleep in the same room as Mama. It is not by choice, and it is not at all what I would wish. In fact, it seems to me altogether wrong.'

I took the liberty of contradicting her again.

'It is quite common. Many poor children have to sleep in the same bedroom as their parents.'

'I am not a poor child.' She was playing a passage for right hand alone, and with her left hand she reached down and pulled at the stuffing that was protruding from her piano stool. 'Though you might think I was for the way we live . . . But the fact is that the moment I go to bed I sleep incred . . . incredabally soundly, though I try not to, and always have every intention of staying awake to see if anything happens.'

'I am glad Your Royal Highness sleeps well. It is the basis of all good health.'

'But not at all the right quality for a good investigator,' she said, giggling.

'I do not see myself staying up all night on observation duty,' I assured her. 'I was very tired last week when I went to Windsor to play for the King and Queen.'

She played a wrong note in her interest at this news, but it was not noticeable among so many.

'You played for the King? That must have been . . . interesting. I shouldn't think his comments were much to the purpose.'

This was said unmaliciously, as a statement of fact.

'I improvised on a hornpipe in His Majesty's honour,' I said. 'He seemed to think I had composed the tune myself.'

'Whereas in fact it is even older than you, Mr Mozart?'

'Even older. It is what is known as "traditional",' I said gravely.

'Young Mr Mendelssohn came to Kensington Palace to play for us last year,' said the Princess Victoria. 'Such a lovely young man – so handsome, and kind, and sympathetic. And people say he's been a musical genius for years and years and years. Were you ever a child progeny, Mr Mozart?'

'I was the most gifted child prodigy the world of music has ever known,' I said magisterially. She giggled again.

'I know you were.' She amended this, unconscious of the insult, to: 'I know that's what you think . . . You do know I tease you a little, Mr Mozart?'

'I know that very well, Your Royal Highness.'

'It's very nice to have an old man I can tease a little.'

'To tell you the truth, it's rather nice to have a young lady who teases me, my dear.'

She played on again, concentrating because she wanted something out of me, making fewer mistakes and managing to get much more of feeling into her playing.

'Tell me what the King says about Me,' she said at last.

I pondered. We had discussed the Princess and her mother at some length after his extraordinary request.

'His Majesty wishes to get to know you better.'

'And I him! He seems to be a much nicer king than dead Uncle George . . . Though perhaps not king*like.*'

'There are different sorts of king, my dear. Many people thought the old King your grandfather was not kinglike. That's why they called him Farmer George.'

She was interested at this. She seemed to want to hear about a King who was a different kind of king to the ones she had known.

'*Did* they? I found an old book of his in the library the other day, one he had when he was Prince of Wales. It was Shakespeare. I . . . I read bits of *Hamlet*. I expect you can guess the bits I was looking for. He had written in the margin: "Such stuff!"'

'He was a very good man,' I said, 'but nobody thought he had impeccable literary taste.'

'I don't think he did. Because I found it terribly exciting. Just to read it made my heart thump like anything. It was very passionate, and very *wise* . . . How will the new King get to know me better?'

'We talked about that,' I said, feeling I had really been mingling with the great. 'He is hoping to ask you and your mother to spend a few days at Windsor – have something of a party.'

She almost stopped playing in her excitement, but just controlled herself, and threw a glance over her shoulder at the sleeping Späth, terrified of having wakened her.

'Oh, that would be wonderful!' she said, in an excited whisper. 'I *should* so enjoy that! Mama *must* let me go. I shall *make* her let me go!'

I coughed warningly.

'May I suggest, my dear, that you do not show too much excitement, do not press your Mama too hard.'

She gave me an interested-to-learn look.

'How *should* I go about it, Mr Mozart?'

'Be very quiet. Say you think you ought to go, because the new King is very popular, and people will be critical if his friendly overtures to his heir are rejected.'

She smiled happily.

'How *wise* you are, Mr Mozart!'

'There is no warranty that it will work. People and their reactions can never be predicted. But it will be more likely to than if you were to show too much enthusiasm.'

'I feel in my bones you are right. You understand Mama even though you have barely met her. Mama is very obstinate. Perhaps I get it from her, just a little. We are alike, but we pull in different directions . . . I am *terribly* tired, Mr Mozart. Can't you play a little, to show how it should go?'

'If Your Royal Highness *listens*. Really listens. We have talked quite enough.'

And there the conversation effectively ended. Soon after I began to play the Baroness Späth nodded awake as suddenly as she had nodded off, and said. 'How beautiful! *Schön!* What wonderful improvement! . . . Oh, Mr Mozart. But of course if you are playing I would have expected—'

'I always play the piece my pupil is practising at the end of a lesson,' I said smoothly. 'To show them what they should be aiming at. But you are quite right, Baroness: the Princess's playing is much improved.'

As the lesson ended, and before I bowed myself out, the Princess whispered, 'What are you going to do next?'

'Never fear, my dear, the matter is well in hand,' I muttered, bending to replace the music in my bag. 'Enquiries will begin immediately.'

As a matter of fact that was true. As I had been shown in by the oafish footman I had questioned him very casually about where his preferred drinking place was, and when he would be off duty. When noises were heard from the dining room he had given me a knowing look, and before he had withdrawn to fetch the Princess and her duenna had said, 'See you there!'

Thus I was to be found later that evening at the Royal Orange, a public tavern ten minutes from the palace, having dined at a detestable chop house where I was not known and where I was forced to pay with ready money. The Royal Orange was clearly the resort of stable-hands and footmen, and was noisy and dirty, but they were nevertheless not unused to a better sort of customer as well, and they served an excellent, tangy ale.

He came at ten past seven, suggesting that he had downed tools at the palace precisely at the time he had told me, seven o'clock. Indeed, since he was wearing an open shirt with a neckcloth, and rather natty grey pantaloons, he must have changed in his employer's time. The British workman! He appeared behind my chair, and said cheerily, 'A pint of the Peculiar, if you're doing the calling, Mr Mozart.' (How I hate that pronunciation, Mo-zart, so unlike the Princess's pretty enunciation of Moat-Zart), and when I returned with his tankard he was sitting confidently on the bench of my snug, looking up at me cockily.

'Your 'elf, Mr M.,' he said, taking a first, long swig.

He was, in his own clothes, not ill-looking. There was the slightest suspicion of a squint in his eyes, but otherwise it was a well-formed face, and his own hair was an attractive brown, much preferable to an askew wig. I could imagine him capturing many hearts below stairs. I could also imagine him in twenty years' time, double-chinned and pot-bellied, as the proprietor of just such an establishment as we were now drinking in – if, that is, he found himself in the meantime a post more likely to yield rich pickings than the Duchess of Kent's service in Kensington Palace.

'Yours,' I responded equably, 'Mr – er—'

'Dorkle. Ned Dorkle. And likewise Yours again.' And he took another long draught of ale. It was going to be an expensive conversation. He licked his lips. 'Lovely drop of ale, this. I always asks for Landlord's Peculiar.'

'Always?' I was surprised into asking.

'When there's gentlemen after information. Like gentlemen from the morning papers. Wery interested in anything they can pick up, the gentlemen from the papers are. Likewise there's even been gentlemen from the Parisian hillustrated magazines – if you can call a Frenchman a gentleman, which I beg leave to doubt.'

'After information about the Princess?'

'Natcherly. What else? That's why it's better to work for the Duchess than for the Princess Sophia, say, for all that she's daughter of a king. Nobody's interested in an elderly princess, whereas everyone's interested in a young one who's going to be the next Queen, God willing. So what you don't get in wages – and you *don't*, believe you me – you make up for in liquid form 'ere.'

He suited actions to words and made up for it in liquid form at my expense.

'And what do you tell these gentlemen?'

He leaned back on his bench, replete with self-approval.

'Nuffink. Precisely nuffink. At great length. I say she's "sweet", "ever so bright", that there's "no side to 'er" – things like that. Also "devoted to 'er muvver", which as I suspect you've realised, Mr Mozart, is not strictly true, but then troof is what those gentlemen wouldn't appreciate if it took their pencils and wrote their pieces for them.'

'Do they use your information, such as it is?'

'Oh yers,' said Dorkle complacently. 'I'm a "source close to Kensington Palace", or "a friend of the Duchess's" as often as not. Oh yes, they goes away and prints it all, and the magazines in Paris prints a hengravin' of a little girl, which could be any little girl and is probably the heditor's daughter, and everybody's 'appy. Now, you're different, Mr Mozart – I can tell that.'

'I should think so.'

'I can see you're not going to be rushing into print. I'm not going to ask why you're after information, because I know you wouldn't tell me. So just fetch me another and tell me what it is you wants to know.'

So there I was, waiter to a footman! I fetched two more pints from the counter and sat down again.

'How long have you been at the palace?' I began.

'Six mumfs. It's not a bad billet, if you can keep cheerful. The Princess is the best thing there. We play 'opscotch in the back yard now and then.'

'What are your impressions of the Princess? Her character, I mean.'

Something like enthusiasm animated his whole body.

'She's a corker! Sharp as a bowie-knife, clever wiv it, and funny into the bargain if she chooses. Oh, she's a spanker! We'd all do anything for Wicky!'

I suspected that if the Duchess had heard him he'd have got his dismissal on the spot.

'You say "sharp". Do you think that if she gets an idea she's probably right?'

He looked more dubious.

'Oh, well, I wouldn't say that, quite. I mean, she's a little girl, i'n't she? Findin' 'er way, like. She'll find it, but she isn't there yet. Couldn't be. See 'ow they've protected 'er. Built a bleedin' great wall around 'er. 'Ardly knows any nippers 'er own age – apart from Sir John's family, wot she can't abide. No, I wouldn't go so far as to say she's always right. It's only natural she gets things wrong now and then.'

'And what's your opinion of the Duchess?'

He screwed up his face, decidedly less enthusiastic.

'Our of 'er depth, if you ask me,' he said, for all the world like an elder statesman. 'Oh, nice enough woman in 'er way. Everyone says she made a good wife to the dead Dook, whatever that may mean – probably that she asked no questions about 'is past so's she was told no lies. You needed to 'ear no hevil and see no hevil if you married one o' that lot.

Ask the present Queen. But I'd say the Duchess is out of 'er depth.'

'In what way?'

'Bringin' up the *h*eir to the throne. She's got a hobsession about it, like it was different to bringin' up any uvver sort o' nipper. Wicky's a bright child, but she's still a child like any uvver. She needs company, she needs to play and 'ave a good time. But she don't. If you ask me, the Duchess 'as gone wrong wiv Vicky, and she won't never go right.'

'And Sir John, and her relations with him?'

His face was suddenly wreathed with a cunning smile, which had lasciviousness mixed in.

'You know, I fort you was going to ask me that, Mr Mozart. Not even the gentlemen from the Paris magazines 'ave come straight out and asked about that: they know about Sir John, but they aren't game to ask. Well, here's what we in the servants' quarters think. If they do it in the palace they're so clever about it that they've never been caught out nor left any hevidence.'

'Elsewhere, then? Sir John's quarters?'

'Sir John 'as a family. Wouldn't 'ave been easy. Elsewhere in London? 'Ired rooms, maybe? An 'otel? It's possible. Opinion is divided in the servants' quarters.'

'I see. What is below-stairs opinion of Sir John?'

He answered without hesitation.

'Below-stairs opinion of Sir John is not divided. He is a shifty indiwiddle. Plausible, smooth, clever in the short term.'

'But not the long?'

'If 'e was clever in the long term 'e'd keep in with 'er nibs the Princess, wouldn't 'e? Instead 'e gets right up 'er nose. Pinning 'is 'opes on a Regency for the Duchess. That begs a lot of questions, as anyone 'oo's seen the King and knows he's a pretty healthy indiwiddle could tell 'im.'

'I take your point. It had occurred to me. And what about his honesty?'

He wiped his mouth and drained his tankard.

'I'd trust 'im about as far as I'd trust your average Member o' Parliament. Wenial, that's what they are, and wenial that's what 'e is. Mind you, I've no hevidence. But ask yourself this: where does the money go? Does it go on servants' wages? Don't make me laugh! On furnishings for the palace? You've seen it. Clothes for the little girl or 'er muvver? They could be a country squire's womenfolk. And the same goes for the poor silly Princess Sophia. He 'as the 'andling of 'er financial affairs too. And a great deal too much 'andling goes on, if you ask me. I wouldn't give 'im the 'andling of my spare change.'

'It was something I'd asked myself about,' I admitted. 'By the way, the King wants to ask the Princess and her mother to Windsor in the near future.'

The footman whistled.

'I fort 'e might. They've fort about it too.'

'What will their reaction be?'

'They'll resist till they're black and blue. Fink up all sorts of hexcuses.'

'Such as?'

'Well, the FitzClarences for a start. You don't 'ave to look far for a good hexcuse, if that's what you're after.'

'She can hardly refuse to meet the King's daughters, who are all married into good families.'

'Don't you believe it. It's their berf she objects to, and a good marriage doesn't alter that. "'Ow can I teach my dear daughter the difference between wice an' wirtue if she is forced to mix wiv the Hillegitimate Hoffspring of the present King?" – you can guess the kind of thing she'll say.'

He jiggled his tankard on the rough table between us, and I went to fetch him another pint, together with something small and stronger for myself. I was in any case humming and hahing to myself, because I suspected that the man was right.

'What, I wonder,' I said as I set the mug and glass down on the table, 'might tip the balance in favour of their going?'

''Ave you thought of money?' he asked, supping deep. I stared at him. It was so obvious I hadn't thought of it. Me, for whom money is so constant and pressing a need.

'Of course. What a fool I've been.'

'The King says he's hanxious to up their Civil List pension, to take account of the fact that Wicky is now *heir* to the throne. Carriages ordered quicker than blinking.'

He had all the right terms off pat. Probably they talked about little else in the servants' quarters.

'I think you're right . . . Mind you, it's a pity: it would probably be money straight into Sir John's pocket.'

'Maybe,' he said shrugging. 'Mind you, women 'ave been known to get over their hinfatuations. If they 'ave a bit more she might be inclined to ask where it's going . . . Mr Mozart.'

He was leaning forward, a worried expression on his face.

'Yes?'

'Is this wise?'

'I beg your pardon.'

'Is this wise, getting Wicky over to Windsor?'

He seemed genuinely worried, and I liked him much more for it.

'I don't see why not. She herself is wild to go. You said yourself the poor little thing has hardly any company.'

'I meant company of 'er own age, not elderly huncles and the breeding cattle they married when they thought there was a chance of providing the *h*eir to the throne.'

'True. Some of them are not company anyone would choose. But it will be a bit of excitement for her.'

'Maybe a sight too much.'

'What do you mean?'

'Have you met Anne Hattersley, Wicky's maid?'

'No. I'd like to.'

'Maybe I can arrange it. She's worked for royals most of 'er life. Says there's a strain of madness there.'

'Well, the old King being as he was, that's not a particularly original observation.'

'Running right through . . . Think of the Duke of Cumberland. Suddenly goes raving mad and takes a razor to 'is own valet.'

'Oh, that was never proved.'

'Doesn't go down well in the servants' quarters, I can tell you.'

'I suppose not. But what are you trying to say, Ned?'

'I'm saying I think she might be in danger.'

FIVE

That Is The Question

I wrote to the new King at Windsor, asking for a meeting to discuss how to persuade the Duchess of Kent to let her daughter attend the family gathering there. I could of course have committed my thoughts to paper, but I wished to make my importance to royalty as open and visible as possible. Already on the news of the favour shown me by the new King there had been performances of several of my old works and promises of more, as well as enquiries about new ones. Bradford – dear Bradford! – had written suggesting a commission for an oratorio. I wasn't very keen on an oratorio. Haydn had done the Creation, Handel had done Jesus Christ – I didn't think there was much left that was commensurate with my talents. The Ten Commandments are so negative. I wrote suggesting a Mass, but they replied saying it smacked of Popery.

Anyway, the King came up trumps (I was beginning to like him already). One of his many grandchildren was having a birthday, and he wondered whether I could put together a little play with music for her. It was the work of half an hour, and I was down to the Queen's Theatre to engage three or four singers for the entertainment. Unfortunately the dreadful old Popper (who is showing his years, and many more) insisted on coming with us, but in spite of this the little piece went capitally. We did it in one of the Drawing Rooms, without any stage or curtain, but I think the children liked us being so close. It was very childish, as it should be, and I think the King enjoyed it even more than his grandchildren. When the birthday party was well under way we withdrew and discussed the gathering of family and friends that he had set his heart on.

The King thought it a capital idea that, along with the invitation to the Duchess her daughter there should go a letter suggesting that during the two or three days he or one of the court officials would discuss with her a substantial increase in her civil list pension ('if Parliament approves,' he put in: 'we have to say that. They're the masters now.') He even agreed that success would be more likely if Sir John Conroy was also invited ('Damned scoundrel though he is'). We thought that if her pension was substantially increased the Duchess might agree to have a separate adviser appointed to run her finances. At the very least Sir John, I suggested, could be subjected to a searching discussion with the Lord Chamberlain about his present conduct of the Duchess's and the Princess Sophia's financial affairs. It might make him more wary of robbing them in the future.

'Damned good idea!' said the King. 'You've got a head for money matters, Mr Mozart.'

'I have had to have, Your Majesty,' I replied. 'I've never had enough of it.'

'I know the feeling. I've never had enough of it either.'

It showed one of the nice sides of the King's nature that after the performance he had invited the actors and actresses (and even Mr Popper) to join the party and partake of all the good things on offer along with the children and their parents. As we rejoined the party he surveyed the jollity with satisfaction.

'Always liked actors and actresses,' he said happily.

The latter preference was hardly news. It was at that point that I should have raised the Duchess's likely objections to the FitzClarences meeting her daughter. But my heart failed me. There the FitzClarences all were around us, and the King was so happy, and would probably have gone apoplectic and said, quite justifiably, that he'd invite who he damned well pleased to his own castle. In any case, at that point he turned to me and said, 'We'll do it again!'

'I beg your pardon, Your Majesty?'

'We'll do it again, for little Victoria. Have a play of some kind – something that an older child would like. I'd wager she doesn't get taken often to the theatre.'

'My impression is, sir, that she's never been taken at all.'

'Good Lord! What a terrible thing! We didn't have much of a childhood, but we did often get taken to the theatre.'

So there we were, with another Royal Command Performance in prospect. Reluctantly I took His Majesty over to Mr Popper, who was pop-eyed, and we began to go into details. We fixed on a scaled-down version of an old piece, *Victor and Victoria*, to be done with an orchestra of six or seven, and with five singers. Ideal. Providing employment for musicians and good publicity for Popper's theatre which, when all was said and done, was *my* theatre too. Popper was in his seventh heaven, and on the way home, inflamed by good wines and rich food, he treated me with something like respect. That had happened before, and it had always ended in tears. One had to savour the moment and build no hopes on it.

I was surprised to receive a few days later, a letter from Kensington Palace, from Sir John Conroy himself in fact, asking if I could make it convenient to come to the palace an hour early for my next lesson with the Princess, as there was a matter of some moment that they wished to discuss with me. 'We', he said – injudiciously I considered. Thinking it over I decided it was unlikely that they wanted to chew over with me the Princess's command of legato, or the unevenness of her scale passages. They had received the letter of invitation from the King and – odd as it might seem – they wished to discuss the matter with me. That could only mean that they had heard of my two visits to the new court at Windsor. I would have become immensely swollen with pride at my new position as confidant and advisor to royalty if I had thought they would genuinely confide in me or even consider my advice. However I didn't.

I was shown by Ned Dorkle into the same shabby sitting room as on my first visit to the Princess, and was met by the same line-up: Sir John, the Duchess, and the Princess Sophia. They were all remarkably friendly, as if we had known each other all our lives. Coffee and delicate little cakes were brought in, and in no time we were all sitting down and looking at each other. Someone had to start the business discussion going, and apparently it had been agreed it should be the Duchess.

'Mr Mozart,' she began, 've believe you have the best interests of the Princess Victoria at heart.'

'No one – no one not of her immediate family – could have them more so,' I said, my enthusiasm sincere (and not the less so for being somewhat intermingled with financial considerations).

'That is very gratifying,' said the Duchess, but in a cold voice that did not convey much gratification. 'The fact is that ve have received an invitation from the King – an invitation vich . . . vich . . .'

'Which for a variety of reasons that we need not go into it would be politic and beneficial to the Princess if the Duchess were to accept,' put in Sir John smoothly.

Money, I thought. Sir John's in favour of accepting. He smells cash. I bowed.

'Ve have talked about this before, Mr Mozart,' the Duchess resumed, 'and I made clear my reservations about contacts between the new King and a fresh, innocent young girl like the Princess. These reservations have not gone avay. But there are . . . prudential considerations as Sir John says. I believe, Mr Mozart, you have been tvice to the court since King William succeeded, have played for them?'

'I have indeed, Ma'am.'

'Do tell us!' said the Princess Sophia, almost bouncing in her eagerness. 'I can just imagine what William is like. Pleased as Punch at being King, chattering endlessly to all and sundry, making appallingly tactless remarks and treading on any corns there are to be trodden on, and generally being as unregal as it is possible to be. And Adelaide is sitting around being dreary, I suppose.' A thought struck her, in mid-flow. 'Well, my mother was always thought a dreary little thing when she came to this country, so I'm told. By the time she died she was generally feared as a formidable old dragon. I was afraid of her myself. Not that Adelaide will have time for that. She seems to have been born to be Queen Dowager.'

I had the impression that Sir John would have stopped her rattling on if there had been no stranger present – that even with me there he had to hold himself back. When she came to a stop I left a moment or two's silence, as I considered my reply.

'I think everyone is pleased to have a queen again, and a

quiet, kind, respectable one is all to the good. It is generally agreed that her effect on the new King's behaviour, as well as his finances, has been beneficial.'

'Oh, everyone would agree about *that*,' said the Duchess, but I thought there was an undercurrent of sourness.

'The new King *does* talk a lot, is friendly to everyone, possibly might be thought unkingly,' I resumed slowly.

'They said the same about Papa,' said Princess Sophia. 'I think kingliness is what the King does.'

I bowed again.

'I have to say that the King's friendliness and approachability seem to be generally liked. The late King – for good medical reasons, no doubt – had been more or less invisible to his people for some years—'

'Reasons of vanity more than health,' said the Princess, rather brutally. 'Didn't like people seeing him looking like he did, so fat and old. Poor George. He was good to his sisters. I have to keep telling myself that.'

'All of this means,' I said, 'that the new King is much liked – not just in the streets of London, as everyone knows, but also at court, in good society generally. Only the *very* stuffy and starchy shake their heads. And it is not just a matter of liking: people feel almost protective towards him. They consider he is good-natured, and would not like to see him hurt by a snub.' Seeing the Duchess purse up her lips, I added, 'Since Your Royal Highness asked my opinion, I could only give it honestly.'

'Of course, of course,' she said, but a bit reluctantly. 'Naturally the court now includes the King's children.'

'Yes, it does.'

'It is out of the question for the Princess Victoria to meet the FitzClarences.'

Here was the nub. The way she said it left no room for negotiation, but I had my hopes. In this matter Sir John's interests coincided with the King's. Sir John left the speaking to me.

'Many of the King's daughters have married gentlemen, members of the aristocracy,' I said, meeting the Duchess's disapproving eyes. 'They go everywhere. It would be extremely awkward to insist that the Princess not meet them at court.'

'It is not a question of who they have married, it's a question of who they *are*, who their mother vas.'

I knew Mrs Jordan. A more charming and generous creature never existed. And she had more genius in her smallest toe than this whole Royal Family had in their collected lumpy bodies. I boiled – but well under the surface.

'It is surely a good principle to show disapproval of vice only towards the sinners themselves,' I suggested, 'not to the innocent results of the sin.'

'Even Mama received George FitzClarence after he came back from the French wars,' said Princess Sophia. 'Wonderfully handsome he was then – still is, so I'm told, though I haven't seen him for years.'

'I don't greatly like these loose modern notions,' said the Duchess obstinately, unimpressed by our attempts to soften her moral tone. 'These are bastard children. If I am to show disapproval only of the sinner, vy should I go visiting to the King? In fact I dislike – pardon me, Sophia dear – the whole idea of letting Victoria associate herself with her father's brothers.'

Since the Duchess's own family had a pretty spectacular (and recent) scandal in it, that seemed pretty rich. I also felt in my more charitable moments that – the Prince of Wales apart – the Royal Dukes were notably domestic men who had had the misfortune to fall foul of the iniquitous Royal Marriages Act. However I could find no way of suggesting tactfully that the Duchess's late husband had been notably faithful to his French-Canadian mistress until the need to provide an heir dragged him away from her into the Duchess's arms. Fortunately Princess Sophia intervened.

'We none of us could marry, unless we married royalty. The Continent was shut off by war. What could we do? William was only human, like the rest of us. I think you could swallow a few FitzClarences, my dear.'

I thought it was time to be practical.

'I suggest, respectfully, that if Sir John were to write – so as not to involve you, Your Royal Highness, too directly – and suggest it would be a little overwhelming for the Princess Victoria to meet too many hitherto unknown cousins at once—'

'Cousins!' said the Duchess.

'I know the King is anxious to calm your fears and meet your wishes, no one more so,' I said. 'But he is a man of strong affections and quick temper. It would not do to try to dictate to him on anything.'

'That seems a prudent and sensible course, Ma'am,' said Sir John to the Duchess.

'Particularly as Vicky has to know what a court *is*,' said Princess Sophia, 'before she has to lead one herself.'

'That is in the lap of providence,' said the Duchess, still very tight-lipped. 'It may be that *I* shall be able to teach her by example how a decorous court should be run, so that it is an example to the nation.'

It was time to be blunt.

'All the more reason,' I said, 'not to risk unpopularity at the present time. A regency would be in the gift of Parliament. A Whig parliament might be expected to look kindly on the Duke of Sussex or the Duke of Cambridge – liberal thinkers both – as possible Regents.'

I was voicing the unthinkable. Unfortunately for the Duchess it happened to be true. There was no way she could be sure, in the event of the King's death, that the Regency would be hers. She had been brought up in a sufficiently homely German court to be used to all sorts of people speaking their minds, little though she liked it. After a long pause she simply said, 'Yes.'

I think she may have been merely accepting the awful possibility that Parliament would refuse to make her Regent. But we took it to mean a consent to the Princess going to Windsor.

'That is very satisfactory,' said Sir John, rubbing his hands.

'I'm sure that's right, my dear,' said the Princess Sophia. 'And I shall be there to do any shielding of Vicky that may be necessary.'

The Princess's very poor eyesight made her unlikely to be of much use in guarding Victoria, but her words brought us to a most important subsidiary matter.

'That is a point on which I would like to make a suggestion,' I put in.

'Yes?'

'The Princess will have her personal maid with her— ?'

'Of course.'

'But the maid will inevitably be behind the scenes, as it were – forgive me: I am a man of the theatre and I think in theatrical terms. Your Royal Highness and Sir John will be much occupied, there will be many people to meet, much to talk about – people you *should* talk to, on your first visit to the new Court. I wonder whether the Princess should have someone *else* around her, someone to shield her from . . . unfortunate encounters.'

I wasn't being quite honest here. I was influenced in this suggestion by the words of Ned Dorkle, foolish and alarmist though I had thought them at the time. I did not care in the least about the possibility of the Princess talking with any of the FitzClarences or their offspring – unless of course it was they who constituted some kind of danger. But it was danger I was thinking about, though at the same time the idea of danger to her, at the heart of a brilliant court, anxious to pay homage to her as the heiress presumptive, seemed sheer nonsense. I hoped it was.

'That is an excellent idea,' said the Duchess, thawing.

'Perhaps the Baroness Späth?'

'Späth has gone back to Germany.'

My heart sank. But she was, perhaps, too inclined to somnolence for the job.

'The Princess's governess? You could say she would be continuing with her lessons during her stay.'

'An excellent idea. Lehzen could be with her all the time.'

'And I wonder—'

'Yes?'

'I wonder if Sir John might express the hope that the Duke of Cumberland might not be invited to Windsor at the same time as the Princess. The King and he are on such bad terms that it surely wouldn't give offence. No doubt the sensational newspapers are exaggerating when they talk about his hatred for the single person that stands between him and the throne, but—'

'I don't think they are exaggerating at all,' said the Duchess firmly. 'You are full of excellent ideas, Mr Mozart.'

And there we left it. The lesson that day was watched over by Baroness Lehzen – prim, strong-featured, a woman of rigid principles and devotion to duty. She was not readily to be lulled to sleep. The Princess was boiling over with frustration. When finally the Baroness did nod off for a few moments, she said, 'What are we to do?'

'I will write you notes,' I whispered. 'Be ready to receive them as I change the music on the stand, or when I put my hand over to show you how a phrase should go.'

It was all very cloak-and-dagger, and more than a little absurd. So it was, too, when, as I was leaving the Duchess of Kent's apartments Ned Dorkle whispered, 'Under the copper beeches in ten minutes. The Princess's maid will come.'

I had little idea what a copper beech looked like, but I decided it was probably copper-coloured in its leafage. I made for the splendid specimen a few hundred yards from the palace, and there, soon after, came hurrying a respectably-dressed woman, with an intelligent face that was lined with cares – poverty, perhaps, or great loss were limned there.

'Mr Mozart?'

Her voice was contralto, Scottish, and tinged, even in such innocuous words, with drama. Without needing words we both took ourselves round to the side of the tree that was out of sight of the palace. She looked at me earnestly.

'Mr Mozart, I can only tarry a few minutes. I hearr it's almost sairtain that my little lass is going to Windsor and this grand party?'

'I think I got the Duchess to look more favourably on the idea. The Princess will be pleased.'

'Oh, the Princess will be over the moon!'

'But?' She frowned and shook her head.

'Mr Mozart, you've no idea what a hairmit the little lass has been. Seeing no one her own age, hardly seeing a morrtal soul except her ain mother and her household. It's no natural. It is no way to brring up a future queen!'

'I would agree entirely about that. But isn't this a step in the right direction?'

'All at once, after such an upbrringing, to land her in the middle of a host of fine ladies and gentlemen? Think how bewildered the puir lassie will be!'

'I think the poor lassie has a much stronger head on her shoulders than you give her credit for.'

'Aye, mebbe. But she is but a child. You'll need to shield her, Mr Mozart. Not just from doing anything foolish, but from danger.'

'I really don't think—'

'Aye, from danger! From folk who wish her harm!' There was entering a touch of Mrs Radcliffe into the conversation that I deplored. Aged servants with prophecies of doom and destruction were staples of her novels that I greatly disliked. They were not in my line at all.

'I'm sure you are needlessly worried.'

'Remember there's none of the family that wish her well.'

'Oh, surely *that's* an exaggeration. Apart from the Duke of Cumberland—'

'And none of the King's family wish her well.'

'Oh, but they can't profit by harming her. And the King is good nature itself.'

'Aye. And have you thought about that, Mr Mozart? Mebee it is in the King's good nature that the greatest danger lies.'

With which lugubrious warning she twitched her skirts and hurried back towards the palace.

SIX

Festivities

The King could look quite king-like if he chose.

If he stood quite still, and if you were looking at him from below, and couldn't see the pineapple shape of his head, and if he was wearing, as now, a decoration in the form of a sash across his chest, you could imagine him as a sovereign of the last century, a benevolent despot, loved and respected by his people.

Then he would bustle forward, and he would become a plump, fussy old gentleman in garish fancy dress.

These reflections were prompted by watching the King as he waited for his guests to arrive at Windsor Castle.

'Damned woman, she's late already and not a sign of them coming through the park,' he said. He looked at his wife with affection. 'Edward made a shocking bad choice of wife, that's the truth of it, and I made a damned good one.'

The Queen, who was standing beside him, returned his look and gave him a watery smile.

'If I may make a suggestion, Your Majesty . . .' I ventured. He turned at once towards me, with the utmost good humour.

'Do, Mr Mozart. Everything you've suggested so far has been damned sensible – eh, Adelaide? You've got a sharp brain in your head, anyone ever told you that? I intend to be guided by you this whole visit.'

I had no illusions that he intended any such thing, or that if he did it would last more than a minute. But I tried.

'I suggest that when the Duchess and the Princess arrive, Your Majesties should receive them as formally, as regally, as possible. I suspect that Your Majesty's instinct would be to go down into the courtyard, give the Princess a hug—'

'Certainly it would, eh, Adelaide?'

'It would, it would, William. I honour you for it.'

'But children like the *idea* of a king,' I went on determinedly. 'Even a little girl who is a princess and who will one day be Queen likes the thought of meeting a real king. She is too old for fairy tales, but she reads her Shakespeare, and the idea of kingship will excite her. But the important one is the Duchess. The more familiar you are to her, the more she will think she can take liberties. The more remote and king-like you are, the more – forgive the plain speaking about your sister-in-law – she will be *shamed* into good behaviour.'

The King drew his finger across his nose, a habit he had when in a state of doubt or anxiety.

'It'll be damnably difficult, eh, Adelaide? We'd like to be a second father and mother to the little girl.'

'I think Mr Mozart is right,' put in the Queen, gently but forcibly. 'You must try to *enforce* a proper respect for the Crown. The Duchess has never behaved respectfully to her English relatives.'

'She does not speak of them respectfully,' I ventured. 'And she forgets that in her own family there is a scandal—'

'Oh ho!' roared the King, in high enjoyment, slapping his thigh. 'The mother of Ernest and Albert. Frolicsome filly. If I'd been her husband I'd have given her a jolly good spanking, not let her bolt off with her . . . Well, well, least said. We take your point, Mr Mozart. We'll do as you say.'

And there we left the matter. I was not hopeful of my advice being followed.

I had arrived at the castle that morning, which I had spent rehearsing the actors for *Victor and Victoria*. In the early afternoon they, and Mr Popper, had returned to London for the evening performance at the Queen's (to the great regret of the King, who clearly enjoyed their company more than he enjoyed the company of his courtiers). My joy at seeing the back of Mr Popper was tempered by the knowledge that he would be returning for the performance next day, though for all he would contribute to it he could better have stayed away.

The Duchess and her party arrived an hour and a half late, by which time all the other guests were in the castle, including George FitzClarence and his children and the Errolls, the two

53

families of the King's natural children who were invited to the gathering. The Duchess and the Princess were shown to their rooms by the castle's flunkeys (a decidedly chastening experience, as I knew to my cost). They only emerged from their apartment and came down to be received by the King half an hour before dinner.

King William was warned of their approach by a sign from the footman at the door. He disengaged himself from a bundle of little FitzClarences and Errolls and stood in the centre of the room to receive his niece and his sister-in-law. The Grand Reception Room gradually fell silent. The Duchess, holding the Princess by the hand, was advancing into the room with apparent confidence, then seemed to lose it a little as she saw the King and Queen standing in the middle of the room, with everyone silent and space made for them to come forward and pay their respects. She swallowed and proceeded forward, clutching her daughter who was wide-eyed and clearly both intimidated yet enjoying herself. When they reached the King and the Queen the Duchess curtsied, and the Princess quite theatrically followed suit. The King broke down.

'Wonderful to see you, my dear!' he said, bending down to kiss his niece, and obviously wanting to heave the doll-like little thing up into his arms to swing her over his head. 'We don't see enough of you, not by a long chalk!' He turned to her mother, and kissed her. 'We are very pleased you have come, my *dear* Victoria.'

It was the first time I had heard anybody call her by her name. Mostly people close to her called her 'Duchess', to avoid confusion with her daughter, who had been called after her. It was, in my view, a most unfortunate choice of name for a princess close to the throne. Who could imagine a Queen Victoria? Elizabeth or Mary would have been much more suitable.

Queen Adelaide behaved admirably, as in her dowdy way she generally did. She kissed the Duchess, then took the Princess a little aside for a chat. After a minute or two she led her over to introduce her to the other children in the room. The Duchess's face darkened, but she was held in conversation by the King, and she had been sufficiently awed by the formality

54

of his initial reception of her to make no protest. Mere tact, I suspected, would not have made her hold her tongue.

The Duchess had delayed her entry so long that there was little opportunity for parleying before it was time to go in to dinner. This was probably going to be her strategy for the whole visit. The King led her in to dinner (a compliment she gave the impression she could very well have done without), and the Queen was taken in by George FitzClarence, a fact which gave a fleeting expression of satisfaction to his handsome, brooding face. The children were taken off to eat elsewhere, but, by a happy touch which I suspect he often displayed where children were concerned, the King had decreed that Princess Victoria was to eat with the grown-ups, and had given her a companion to sit beside her: the young Prince George of Cambridge. Since he was the only one of the King's brothers to have led a blameless life, this boy's father, the Duke of Cambridge, was put at the Duchess of Kent's side at the top of the table, so she had nothing to complain about, beyond, probably, the rambling and scurrilous nature of the King's conversation.

I was, of course, seated in a position of great obscurity, if any position in the Waterloo Chamber could be regarded as obscure. Even so I was surrounded by people who wondered why I was there at all. It had its advantages, however. For example, Sir John Conroy was three places up on the other side of the table, and when talk died down around me (as it frequently did, since none of the people by whom I was surrounded had anything in common with each other), I could hear his conversation with Lord Howe, the new Queen's Chamberlain.

'The Duchess wants for the Princess a simple, natural upbringing,' he said, over the fish. 'Far from pomp, grandeur, formality.'

'I see,' said Lord Howe, a chilly figure, so remote as to be almost inhuman, and wrapped in a stately formality which seemed to belong to another age. 'And for companionship?'

'She has my own children. And . . . and selected children, from time to time.'

'I see.' Lord Howe gave no impression of disapproval, but added, 'It is to be hoped that the Duchess will gradually introduce her to polite society. The King is not a young man, nor as healthy as he looks. She will need to know something of it before she becomes its Head.'

An obstinate expression came over Sir John's face.

'She will have natural tastes and strong moral principles to guide her,' he said. 'You may trust the Duchess's instincts. She has been a mother before.'

'Ye-e-erse,' said Lord Howe, returning to his fish.

Lowly as my position at table was, I could from time to time get a view of the great ones. I could see the Princess Victoria conversing solemnly with Prince George, both of them being quite desperately grown-up. He was a good-looking boy of her own age, and when the Princess was not stealing glances at the grand company that surrounded her (which was rather difficult, as they were more often than not stealing glances at *her*) I saw her looking thoughtfully at her young companion, sizing him up, I suspect wondering if he was *husband* material. I also saw the Duchess of Kent throwing worried looks in the direction of her daughter. I felt sure that the King's happy thought of letting his niece mingle with his court had been an unpleasant surprise for the Duchess. If she had had her way her daughter would stay a child for ever.

I could also contrast the behaviour of two of the FitzClarences. The King's daughter, the beautiful Countess of Erroll, surrounded by the nobility and notables of the court, talked, laughed, gossiped unaffectedly, as if she were born to court life. She acted not as a princess, but as one who had no doubts about her place among the country's great and powerful.

Her brother, George FitzClarence, was seated between the Queen and the Princess Sophia. The Queen from time to time talked earnestly to him, and the Princess was clearly delighted with his good looks and his impressive presence: she flirted with him outrageously, quite unworried by the difference in age. FitzClarence himself said little, but whenever anyone around him addressed any remarks directly to him, his manner took on an air of prickliness, mingled with self-regard, a desire to assert his position. His unease in society detracted from the natural effect of his handsomeness and air of distinction. He was, in short, all too aware of his position as King's son and not King's son.

As dinner drew to a close, King William rose. Queen Adelaide immediately began to look worried. Gradually a hush descended on the tables. The King swayed, but gently. He was not drunk, only happy.

'No speeches,' he began. 'Except mine. Privilege of kingship, what? And mine won't be long. This is a family occasion. Family and friends. No call for speeches. But I want to bid a special welcome tonight to my brother Edward's widow, and her damned fine daughter. I can't tell them what pleasure it gives the Queen and me to see them here tonight.' He was in his stride. The Queen looked even more worried. The Duchess's expression said as clearly as words that she would very much have preferred not to be singled out. 'I remember something m'friend Lord Nelson once said. Wasn't Lord then, of course. Captain then. Finest man I ever knew in my life. Model for the country's youth in every way.' The Duchess pursed her lips, as if to convey that she could think of a respect in which Lord Nelson was no model at all. 'And if I say he was the finest man this county has produced in my lifetime, by God I defy any other country to produce finer men than British men!' General murmur. A king's patriotism doesn't have to be subtle. The Queen cleared her throat. 'And what Nelson said to me was "A victory at arms gives a man a damned good feeling, but ..." Ah no. Perhaps not. Not suitable. But the gist of it was that a damned fine girl makes you feel even better.' The Queen cleared her throat again, much more loudly. 'Ah – you're right, my dear. Quite right. I've gone on long enough. I remember m'late brother once said to me – no. Time for a toast. I give you the Duchess of Kent and her damned fine daughter!'

There was an enthusiastic rising and compliance with the toast. The Princess looked uncertainly at her mother to see if she should rise, but otherwise behaved very prettily. There was no mistaking the singling out of her, not just by the King but by all present: if her mother thought she remained ignorant of her closeness to the throne after this then she would be badly underestimating her daughter's intelligence.

I withdrew quite soon after the ladies. All-male society does not appeal to me – in fact the King's conversation was a bit too all-male for quite a number of his guests, including the Queen's Chamberlain Lord Howe, who withdrew tight-lipped as if he had never heard a risqué story in his life. In the Grand Salon the Princess Victoria was watching the refugees from table, and came up to me at once.

'Did I do satisfactorary?' she asked.

'You did wonderfully well.'

'My cousin was a bit of a burden to have to talk to for so long. He is rather good-looking, in fact decidedly so, but he is *very* boring.'

'Very few men unite good looks with high intelligence, Your Royal Highness.'

'Is that not sad? And when I choose my husband it has to be someone of royal birth as well. How very difficult that makes things! Never mind. Some day my Prince will come. Meanwhile I must enjoy such days as this when they come my way . . . Oh.' She had turned away from me, to greet a passer-by. 'You are my cousin, are you not? I am Princess Victoria.'

It was the Countess of Erroll. Close to she was even more lovely than she had seemed across the table of the dining room, and quite enchanting of manner. My heart gave a lurch as I remembered her mother in her early days in the theatre. Mrs Jordan was a woman and an actress in a thousand, and rather wasted, in my view, on a royal duke.

'I am indeed your cousin, and very happy to make your acquaintance, Your Royal Highness,' she said, curtsying grace-fully. 'I have long hoped for the pleasure. May this be the first of many visits you pay to Windsor.'

'I hope so, but I don't think it likely,' said Victoria, with her usual directness. 'Mama is very insistent that I be brought up simply and naturally. It is probably very good for me, but it is terribly dull as well.'

She threw a look in her mother's direction. The Duchess was deep in conversation with the Duchess of Cambridge, another minor German princess and mother of the dull boy. If her mother had not been preoccupied, I felt sure that the Princess would not have been so daring as to introduce herself to her bastard cousin.

'I can imagine life being brought up naturally and simply could be extraordinarily dull,' said the Countess gaily. 'But I could imagine you getting a great deal of fun working *around* the rules, cousin.'

'Some,' admitted the Princess, with a brief wicked smile. 'But the possibilities are limited. Now I shall go and thank George Cambridge for his company at dinner, tedious though it was, and then go to bed, because if I don't, tomorrow Mama will say that after such dreadful diss . . . dissipations I should have lessons the whole morning.' She flashed her funny pig-smile at her cousin. 'Can you imagine wasting any moment of a wonderful experience like this by doing *lessons*?'

As she went in the direction of Prince George the Countess whispered to a footman that the Princess was about to go to bed. When Victoria came back I bowed to her and escorted her to the stairs and bade her goodnight. She looked happier than I had ever seen her. As she toiled up the staircase Mrs Hattersley appeared in the mysterious way that servants have, and escorted her through the magnificent corridors to her room.

I lingered in the shadow of the stairway, uncertain whether I wanted to go back among the glittering throng. Glittering they might be, but there wasn't one among them I was confident of securing a loan from, should I broach the matter. As I considered, the last men were coming from the direction of the Waterloo Chamber. With a shock I realised it was the King and his eldest son. The King was a little unsteady on his feet, and his voice was thick. George FitzClarence was not unsteady at all. I stayed in the shadow, not wishing to be an eavesdropper, but not wishing either to intrude on father and son. The voices made a dull rumble in the vastness of the castle, until at last they were only a few feet away and words became plain.

'My dear boy, you know I love you very much, but you are always asking, always wanting.'

'No more than my due, Papa, no more than my proper place.'

'Difficult things to decide, those.'

'Not difficult at all, Papa.'

'Dear boy, you have too keen a sense of your wrongs. You ask, ask, ask. What can I do that would content you?'

George FitzClarence's next words were hissed, so I could not be sure that I heard them correctly. Even if they had been spoken aloud I doubt I would have believed the evidence of my ears.

'What can you do, Papa? *Make me Prince of Wales!*'

SEVEN

Gunshots

The next morning I was very busy. I had been so exhausted the night before that I slept well, though in the waking moments that I did have my mind buzzed with that absurd demand of George FitzClarence that I had overheard in the shadow of the stairs: 'Make me Prince of Wales!'

But almost from sunrise I was too preoccupied for these words even to cross my mind. I was supervising the setting up of a stage in the Grand Reception Room. There had been theatricals there in the old King's time (the theatre was about the only human weakness of Queen Charlotte, apart from fecundity), and a rudimentary stage with curtains existed, which King William had remembered and caused to be resurrected from some distant lumber-room. The garden staff who were charged with its erection were willing but inexpert. The musicians and actors, along with Mr Popper, arrived from London around eleven, and one or two of them 'helped' – that is, got in the way, contradicted my directions, ridiculed the gardeners' efforts and so on. The rest, led by a fawning Popper, mingled with their betters in the castle or the park.

On the rare occasions when I needed to go to other parts of the castle (mostly to require something of the footmen, who were unhelpful in the extreme) it seemed swarming with people. On one such occasion I came upon Princess Victoria and her governess Baroness Lehzen, together and talking animatedly in a corner of the Crimson Drawing Room.

'De Princess is not inclined to her lessons,' explained Lehzen, her plain face lighted by suspicious little eyes.

'It's all so *interesting*,' said the Princess, her own eyes sparkling

61

and frank. 'How can I miss what is an education in itself? Oh, Mr Mozart, do look at Cousin George!'

I looked in the direction of her gaze. The young Prince George of Cambridge, all of eleven, was talking to Hetty Forbes, who played the secondary role of Anne in our piece that afternoon. Hetty had a weak voice but she more than passed muster because she was enchantingly pretty and unaffectedly jolly. Prince George was fixing her with a look of besotted admiration. Princess Victoria regarded him, in her turn, with fascination.

'Look at him! Isn't it wonderful? He can't take his eyes off her. And she is *lovely*, isn't she? And charming too. Oh, I wish I looked like that! That really is what they mean when they talk of love, isn't it, Mr Mozart?'

'Princess Victoria! The young lady is an actress!' protested Lehzen. I had to conceal a smile.

'I don't think you would say that if the King were by,' said the Princess. 'And it's not very polite to Mr Mozart, who is a man of the theatre. Anyway, some men have a *penchant* for actresses, don't they, Mr Mozart?'

'Quite a lot of men do,' I said solemnly.

'I think cousin George has ... Isn't that a lovely word, *penchant*?' went on the little sprite. 'I don't like to use French words, because it's not patriotic, but there isn't an English one that would do half as well.'

By half-past twelve the little stage, with the elementary set and props which had come with the party from the Queen's Theatre, were up and in place. As I and the garden staff were surveying our handiwork one of the footmen came with a tray, on which was set an elegant little meal, with a glass of wine.

'By order of the King,' he said distantly, to emphasise that, left to himself, he would never have deigned to bring a musician food. He looked like an unfrocked bishop who felt his position keenly.

As I settled down happily to eat, under-footmen began to bring in chairs, supervised by the Bishop himself. When the Grand Reception Room was nearly half full of chairs, and still they kept coming, I went over to him.

'Surely there are enough?' I suggested.

'The King has asked quite a number of extra ... *people*.' His Lordship drew in his breath and spoke as if a grave sin had been

62

committed. He was a large man, with an intimidating paunch, and he seemed born for theological conversations over port. 'For the day. To see the . . . entertainment. And some will be staying on. To dinner.'

He gave the impression that he would shortly be applying for a position with the Marquis of Bath or the Duke of Malborough – someone who knew how to maintain the proper distance and dignity of his position. He had explained the crush of people in other parts of the castle, however.

The performance was due to start about two. Afterwards there were to be refreshments, both inside the castle and outside on the terraces. It had started as a fine day and I had seen the footmen taking trestle tables outside. As people drifted in for the play I noticed that it had clouded over, and they were starting to bring them in again. The King and Queen came in at five to two, he looking around him incessantly and talking to and greeting all manner of people here and there around the improvised theatre. I feared that he would chatter all through the performance, but then I remembered he had been constantly at theatres during his twenty years with Mrs Jordan, and certainly knew how to behave. The Queen smiled graciously at newcomers, then sat down quietly. Four seats had been set aside for her and the King, and the Duchess of Kent and the Princess. These were some five rows back, with a seat on the aisle for the Princess so that she could see better.

'Doesn't do to get too close,' the King explained to her when she arrived only a minute or two before curtain up. 'See all the powder and paint. See they're not as young as they look. No better than they should be, some of these actr – *No*. Pretty little stage, ain't it? M'father had it made, and we spent many happy hours in the audience. Don't make plays like they used to, you know . . .'

And he rattled on till I signalled for the curtains to be drawn to shut out the daylight, and began leading the six musicians in the pretty overture.

About the performance I shall say little. It went with a swing: actors are naturally obsequious, and do their best when performing for an audience from whom patronage of one sort of another is to be expected. The new King's long association with an actress encouraged hopes: no doubt the lower decks of the Navy expected double rations of rum. The theatre people should have remembered that Mrs Jordan died in Paris, deserted and forlorn.

My main pleasure, when my direction of players and singers permitted it, was watching the Princess Victoria. She sat there, her head hardly coming up to the top of the seat-back, her eyes sparkling, her little mouth slightly open. She was totally entranced, and I thought that, if the theatre was to have expectations, they should be addressed to her.

As the piece progressed, during the stretches of dialogue, I was able to take in the audience. There was a smattering of politicians, doubtless invited to give them a rare chance to pay their respects to the heiress Presumptive. The Iron Duke was unmistakable, but I also spotted Lord Grey and Lord Melbourne. I saw the Princess Sophia, rouged, a little haggard, but ineffably charming, and two seats away from her George FitzClarence, seemingly in a world of his own, not only oblivious to *Victor and Victoria* (which was understandable), but oblivious to the fact that the Princess Sophia shot him frequent glances of admiration. Between them was a man who seemed somehow to have found himself mingling with his betters – a man in his thirties, in a shabby brown coat, not ill-looking but with shifty eyes and the air of a scamp. I found myself wondering how he had come to be invited (even, as the footman would say, 'for the day') to Windsor Castle. Was he perhaps a Windsor tradesman to whom the royal household owed a lot of money? Was he another FitzClarence being smuggled in against the agreement with the Duchess of Kent? If so he had none of the distinguished looks or air that the other representatives already there possessed.

I also noticed Prince George of Cambridge. His raptness in the performance was equal to Princess Victoria's, but had a difference: she was enchanted by the play, and he was besotted by Hetty Forbes. As a man of the theatre I recognised the two sides of its appeal. The Prince sat beside his parents, but behind him sat Sir John Conroy and the Baroness Lehzen. The Baroness's eyes were on her pupil, with a fond smile at her reactions to the piece. But Sir John was thoughtful, his laughter automatic, triggered by the reactions of the rest of the audience. I wondered if he had had that talk with the King's Secretary, and was realising that his conduct of the financial affairs of the two royal ladies was about to be subjected to more scrutiny than it could comfortably bear.

The piece had been considerably shortened (it was so trivial this could only be to its advantage), and we brought it to a conclusion not long after three. The audience was unusually enthusiastic for a Royal Command Performance, and the King led them in cheering the actors who basked in curtain calls punctuated by childish cheers. King William and the Duchess led Princess Victoria over to thank me, and after she had done this formally she pulled me aside to express her real opinions.

'Oh, Mr Mozart, it was *won*derful! The most exciting thing I've ever seen in my whole life! If only they could do it all over again.'

'My d – . . . Your Royal Highness,' I resumed, more circumspectly, 'must remember that actors and singers are only human. They need rest. Singers must never strain their voices.'

'Of course. I must not be incon . . . inconsiderate – is that right? But oh! They were wonderful!'

'We must hope that this is the first of many visits to the theatre for you.'

'Oh, I hope so! I must be very sober and serious in my talking about it with Mama and Lehzen. That's the way to manage them, isn't it? But oh, it was so thrilling! And you are a wonderful musician, Mr Mozart. Quite the equal of Mr Mendelssohn!'

On my opening my mouth to protest at this insult she giggled, then followed demurely the rest of the company, who were adjourning to the main Drawing Rooms, where the refreshments that should have been *al fresco* were laid out. The day outside was breezy and changeable, but some of the company had already taken glasses and plates out to the East Terrace. I thought of following suit, but mindful of my pledge to the Duchess I decided to wait to see what the Princess Victoria did. I very much considered myself one of her several guardians. At that moment she was being bowed to and talked to by Lord Melbourne.

'Now Melbourne knows how to talk to a young gel,' said an unmistakable voice at my elbow. I turned and bowed to the King. 'Odd, because he's had damned bad luck with women himself. Should have locked her up, that wife of his – throwing herself at that poet chappie! But a nice man, damned nice feller. I had to ask the Duke of Wellington – Prime Minister and all that – but he's no more idea of how to talk to a child than a brick wall has. If he can't drill and parade them he doesn't know what to do with them.'

'Probably,' I said, 'he was seldom at home when his own children were young.'

'That's it. That's what you have to do – play with them, wipe their noses.' He drew his own finger across his own nose. 'She loved your little piece, Mr Mozart. Enraptured. So was I. Took me back, I can tell you. It was just the piece for a child of that age. Ah – Lord Grey!'

And off he trotted, perpetually perambulating, perpetually chattering. But he had had an effect on court functions. This was a much more relaxed and friendly occasion than his brother had ever managed to hold, even at Brighton, where informality was supposed to rule. If forced to choose between George's stateliness and William's indiscriminate sociability, I would plump every time for the latter. And I would feel confirmed in my choice by the sight of the footman-Bishop, who even as the thoughts were going through my head was gazing at the throng with lofty disapproval, as if the stage-coach had dropped him by mistake in Sodom or in one of Mr Robert Owen's Socialist communities.

My charge was now talking to the Duke of Wellington. In spite of King William's strictures both seemed to be easy and confident, though the physical distance beween his head and hers was immense. Certainly the Princess did not seem overawed. Probably she was telling him how to win battles.

My glance strayed. Princess Sophia was surrounded by men. It seemed as if that was her natural state, which must have made her life under the tyranny of her mother a terrible trial. Sir John Conroy was one of the men, and she was talking animatedly to him, sometimes turning her head to seek agreement from

George FitzClarence, who looked preoccupied – perhaps withdrawn to his dream world where he could be Prince of Wales – and just nodded now and then. There was another man there, but I could only see his back, and it was a surprise a minute or two later to see that the Princess Sophia detached him from the group, and the two of them headed towards the terraces – in his case, I thought, a trifle reluctantly. It was the shifty young man who had been sitting beside her for the play. So he was, presumably, not a discontented tradesman at all. What, I wondered, was he?

These pictures are fixed in my mind by what happened a few minutes later. When I looked back towards the body of the room I saw that the Duchess of Kent was talking to Lord Grey and Lord Melbourne in an unusually friendly and animated way. They had been friends, I remembered, of her late husband, who had trifled with radical notions in his later years. The coming woman and the coming politicians, I thought. It was widely believed that the Duke of Wellington's ministry could not last long, and then the Whigs would come into their own – and perhaps she with them. The Duke, in fact, came over to join the group with the apparently easy friendliness of aristocratic political foes. The Duchess immediately lost the ease and friendliness of her own demeanour. Silly woman, I thought.

Her daughter was being pressed to take wine by the King. The Queen was standing nearby, and immediately tried to dissuade him, but the King in certain moods was not to be deflected, and he took a full glass of claret from a nearby flunkey and pressed it into his niece's hands. She humoured him and sipped it, and was polite enough not to make a face. The King was happy with that, and pottered off, chuckling contentedly.

When the first shot rang out I seemed to jump two feet in the air. So did everyone else. By the time the second shot came all the fine ladies and gentlemen in the room (as well as Mr Popper) were scurrying hither and thither. I darted as fast as my old legs would carry me in the direction of the Princess Victoria, but the Duchess of Kent was younger and faster, and was across the room and in front of her daughter in a trice. She looked grateful for my presence of mind, however, and I turned to the window, for the shot had seemed to come from the terraces or the park beyond. Some in their agitation had hidden behind chairs or sofas, among them Mr Popper, still others had scurried out of the room. After the first shock was over, however, and seeing that no one had been hurt, several of the men and the Countess of Erroll with them had gone over to the windows, and now I went to join them. Gradually more and more, in spite of the continuing gunshots, sensed there was no danger, and went to enjoy the spectacle. Spectacle it certainly was.

On horseback, around the paths that intersected the terrace gardens, rode a fearsome figure in a cavalry uniform I did not recognise, with mutton-chop whiskers covering much of his face and ... Oh God! ... and a vacant eye-socket that gave his face a fearsome appearance. It was when he turned towards us and I saw the socket that I knew who it was, knew it was someone I had had more than enough to do with in my lifetime. As we watched he turned towards the castle, smiling evilly, and raised his pistol again. Bang! And then bang-bang again. In the gardens, I now saw, were the Princess Sophia and the rascally-looking man – he cringing back, she looking on with calm amusement. The horseman rode in their direction, laughed, and then fired again.

'M' brother Ernest,' said the King calmly, from among the ranks of his guests crowded at the windows. 'Damn' fool, as usual. Should be locked away.'

The fearsome figure looked towards the castle once more, threw back his head and laughed a laugh more fearsome than a howl, then turned away from the gaping courtiers, spurred his horse, and rode off in the direction of the great park.

'Thinks he's in pantomime,' said the King, in great disgust. 'Come away and forget him. M' sister-in-law insisted I didn't invite him. That's what this is all about. Only shows how right she was. Very sensible.' She was standing with her daughter just behind him, and he patted her arm and put a hand on Victoria's shoulder. 'Had no intention of inviting him anyway. Don't like him near me. Gives me the horrors. Gives everyone the horrors. Particularly a little gel, eh? Ugly, one-eyed devil looking at her as if he'd like to eat her up? Give her nightmares. So this is what he does. Damn' fool trick. Come along. Don't let it spoil the party. The sun's coming out. Let's go out into the park.'

He took the Queen's arm, and to set an example began towards the terraces. Some followed him, others did not care to risk the possibility of the Duke of Cumberland returning to play an encore. The Duchess of Kent was among the latter. I saw her go over to Sir John Conroy, almost dragging the Princess, and as I drew near, as I took care to, I heard the word 'risk'.

'Here ve vould be imprisoned for the rest of the visit,' I heard the Duchess say, in a low but urgent voice. 'Thankfully the man vould be prevented from entering the castle, especially after this display, but who is to prevent him coming back to the park? The King is right: he should be in Bedlam. I could not let Victoria even take a valk on the terrace.'

Sir John shook his head, dubious.

'There is no sense in that. Kensington Palace is as public as Windsor. The fact that both are so *public* guarantees that no outrage of the kind you fear could take place.'

'But if the man concerned is *mad*— ?'

He bent forward.

'Remember our purpose. With the King in his present benevolent mood we may get a settlement for Victoria beyond our wildest dreams.'

The Duchess was pettish.

'The King is alvays benevolent. He is also feeble-minded, and vould like to treat Victoria as his own. The family has bad blood. With the sole exception of my dear Edvard, all the boys vere either dangerous, mad or simply idiotic. I vant nothing to do vith any of them.'

I turned away from the Duchess's selective genealogy, which had recreated her husband, the Mad Martinet of Gibraltar, as the only Saint and brain in the family. I suspected that Sir John would get his way. I suspected he always did – which brought me back to the Princess's question of what there was between them. They certainly did not talk together as royal mistress and devoted servant.

As I walked over to greet the group of actors and singers from the Queen's Theatre, I saw Mr Popper turn away from another group he was pestering over by the fireplace, put his hand to his stomach, then rush, lurching and stumbling towards the door.

Mr Popper was accustomed to get inebriated after the performance at the Queen's, so I thought nothing of it at the time.

EIGHT
Positively Last Appearance

It is odd that you sometimes know when something that concerns you is happening behind your back. Being by nature a rational person, and no enthusiastic seeker after supernatural explanations, I can only think that on this occasion I saw, without consciously noticing, some reflection in the windows of the Crimson Drawing Room, through which I was watching the King and the other company on the terraces, and further away the figures of the Princess Sophia and her young man, together yet slightly apart, rambling towards the rolling expanses of Windsor Great Park.

Be that as it may, I knew that something was going on, and when I turned round I saw that the episcopal footman was pointing me out to a man in everyday attire – a short, thick-set man, rubbing his hands in distress or as some kind of apology. My immediate thought was that he was a dun or a bailiff (my immediate thought when I see strangers who want to accost me often is), but on reflection I realised that such pests would hardly be allowed to invade a royal reception at Windsor Castle. The man began forward towards me, an expression of great, indeed agonised concern on his face.

'Oh dear, Mr Mozart? My name is Nussey. I am most distressed at having to trouble you at such a time—'

I had rarely encountered such a determined apologist. I said: 'Not at all.'

'—but, hmm, a matter of great . . . great inconvenience renders it imperàtive. Unavoidable. I wonder if you could be so kind as to accompany me?'

I looked about me towards the Princess Victoria. She was with her mother and the Queen's Chamberlain, Lord Howe

– hardly company she would have chosen for herself. I raised my eyebrows to the Duchess, signifying my intention, and then left the room with the decidedly obsequious (it is not often anyone is obsequious to me, so it was rather pleasant) man with the North of England accent. We were followed by my least favourite footman (and I don't like them as a race) up stairs, down corridors, up stairs again. Mr Nussey walked very fast, no doubt not realising (my appearance is still surprisingly youthful) that I am a very old man.

'I should explain, Mr Mozart. I am one of the Royal apothecaries. I attended, I should say,' (his chest expanded) 'His Late Majesty in his last illness.' His self-importance was rather comic, and he looked round to see its effects even as we hurried on. I bowed to hide my face. 'I was here, ministering in fact to one of the royal attendants when I was called for by a footman . . . You know a Mr Popper, I believe?'

'Mr Popper?' I said, my surprise showing on my face. 'We have been long . . . acquainted.'

'And he was – is – here with a . . . a theatre troupe?'

'He is here with a little company from the Queen's Theatre, in Haymarket, who have been entertaining the royal guests,' I said with a hint of reproof. Mr Popper's dignity, on this occasion, was my dignity. 'The King had the idea of staging a little piece to amuse the Princess Victoria and other younger members of the royal family.'

'I see. And you are a member of the troupe?'

I swallowed. On such occasions I always want to tell people that I am the greatest living composer in Europe.

'I directed the performance.'

I tried to remember whether I had written any of the dribble of music the piece contained, but couldn't. Anyway, I didn't want to claim the discredit.

'And did you notice Mr Popper after the performance?'

'I saw him stumble out, obviously drunk. Regrettable, no doubt, but hardly the first time that one of the guests has been drunk at a royal party.'

'We must hope that it is that,' murmured the man dubiously, coming to a stop outside an obscure door. 'We must indeed hope it.'

There were sounds, groans, penetrating the thick wood of the door. He opened it and we both went into a small, mean chamber. On the bed was Mr Popper, in an extremity of pain and distress. Holding his hand, trying to administer an emetic, was a woman I recognised as Mrs Hattersley, the Princess's personal maid. When he opened his eyes and saw me Mr Popper gestured, then collapsed with a terrible cry, holding his stomach.

I had frequently, in the course of our long and aggravating association, wished a terrible death on Mr Popper. He was one of my least favourite persons in the world, and the one I had least reason to be grateful to. But faced with his agony I took it all back, and wished only for his recovery. Even at the first glance, though, I concluded he was in a death agony. I turned to Mr Nussey.

'What has caused this?'

'What indeed?' he asked in reply. 'This is not inebriation. Does he have a weak heart?'

At any other time I would have replied that it would be news to the company at the Queen's that he had any heart at all, but not to the sounds of the groans from the bed.

'I believe there have been occasions recently – I am no longer closely associated with Mr Popper's theatre, so I don't know the details – when he has had palpitations, *turns*, small attacks, call them what you will.'

'Then I fear—'

'Yes?'

'I fear he cannot survive.'

I frowned in something like distress, and I stood for a moment thinking of the course of events since I saw Popper staggering from the Crimson Drawing Room.

'Mr Popper was ill among the company downstairs,' I said. 'What happened after that?'

'He was taken ill at the bottom of the main stairway. The footman' – he gestured in the direction of the Bishop – 'had him brought here.'

'Was there nowhere nearer?'

'Nowhere . . . suitable.'

Nowhere lowly enough to suit the footman's estimation of Popper's place in the universe. I could hardly protest, having had an estimate of him pretty close to the deathwatch beetle myself hitherto. Anyway a dingy death in a grand castle seemed oddly appropriate for a theatre manager.

'I don't quite understand how you came to call on me.'

'He asked for you,' said Mr Nussey, naively adding, 'Mrs Hattersley knew of you, otherwise I would not have been able to understand the name he was trying to pronounce.'

On cue there were renewed calls from the bed.

'Mr Moz . . .'

I went over quickly and almost warmly took his hand.

'Mr Popper, I am most distressed to see—'

'Mr Mozart. It must have been in one of the gl . . . gl . . .'

To my horror his words were interrupted by another terrible cry. Then his head sank back on to the bed and his eyelids looked up to the ceiling as if he was already (unlikely thought) catching his first glimpse of heaven. Mr Nussey elbowed me aside. He felt heart and pulse, then after a minute he stood up.

'It is as I feared.'

'*Dead*?'

'Yes.' The man seemed to be struggling with contrary emotions. 'What was he trying to say?'

I felt I had to voice my suspicions at once.

'It's difficult to tell, but I *thought* he was trying to say "It was in one of the glasses."'

He seemed to make a decision.

'I fear he may have been saying just that.'

'You mean?'

'I think he was trying to say he had been poisoned.'

Now he had shared his own suspicions he breathed a heavy sigh of relief. I sat down in a chair, shocked at what had happened. My years have inured me to catastrophes and deaths, but not, as yet, to murder – my experience of that was limited, though choice.

'But I don't understand,' I said, bewildered. 'What did he mean, "one of the glasses"? He would only have had one.'

There was a stirring by the door. I realised that, lurking in the dim corridor, was the footman who had followed us. He ignored me and addressed himself to Mr Nussey.

'It is possible I can be of assistance, sir.'

'Yes, my man?'

My man! To such a man!

'When the . . . shooting in the terrace garden occurred, most people first hid, or went for cover.' He looked superior, but then it was his habitual expression. 'Then, when people realised it was . . . a royal prank – ' his face became ineffably contemptuous – 'they all crowded over to the windows to see.'

'That is true,' I put in.

'Except this . . . man. When he emerged from behind a sofa he . . . saw there was nothing to be afraid of and . . . went round drinking from glasses. Drinking them down. While everyone's backs were turned.' His voice took on the warmth of contempt. 'As if the King stints on wine for his guests.'

When this had sunk in I stood up in great agitation and went up close to him.

'*Whose?*'

'I *beg* your pardon?'

'Whose glass did he drink from?'

He was supremely frosty at my effrontery.

'Several. I really couldn't tell you which.'

Like other bishops I could name he was very stupid.

'*Where* were the glasses?'

He sighed at my pertinacity.

'Oh, on the fireplace. The small table nearby. On the piano.'

'There was a full glass of claret which the King had given to the Princess Victoria. It would have been on the table near the fireplace, I think. *Did he drink that?*'

At last I had got through to him. His jaw dropped.

'I know he drank one very full glass of red wine . . . Oh, my Gawd!'

There was silence in the room. Mr Nussey stirred by my side. Finally he spoke.

'You realise that this has not happened, Mr Mozart.'

I wheeled round on him.

'I beg your pardon.'

'This has not happened. Murder does not take place in a royal household. I shall sign the death certificate as heart failure. What else was it?'

I grew red and spluttered. For once my duty was plain for me to see.

'Mr Nussey, I *cannot* allow this business to be hushed up.'

He tried to outstare me. He was a man, clearly, who had got where he was by fawning on the great, not by taking a strong moral line.

'You have no choice, sir. You have no medical knowledge, I take it, to contradict my own? I tell you again, murder has not taken place. Think of the King's popularity, the general pleasure his geniality arouses in his subjects. Think of the effect of a murder in his own royal home!' He added, quite unconscious of the bathos, 'My own position would be jeopardised for ever.'

I said with more confidence than I felt, 'Your position will be jeopardised still more, Mr Nussey, if you try to hide the fact that someone has attempted to murder the heir to the throne. The King and Queen are both extremely fond of the little Princess.'

'The King and Queen need know nothing.'

'What if another attempt is made, perhaps successfully made, and the details of this one emerge? Then the King would find out that you covered up the *fact* that Popper died of poison, and that you did it to protect your position in the Royal Household.'

I could see that he was wavering. I pressed home my advantage.

'Quite apart from the fact that, while I may not be able to contradict you on medical matters, I do have privileged access to the King himself.'

He gaped, hardly flatteringly.

'You?'

I turned to the footman.

'Perhaps you will confirm that.'

The Bishop looked as if he were being confronted by a ranting dissenter.

'It . . . seems so. Apparently.'

I turned back to Mr Nussey, and addressed him with the utmost seriousness.

'The matter on which the King has consulted me is not

unrelated to – to this.' I waved my hand in the direction of the bed, which I preferred not to look at, though I was conscious that Mrs Hattersley was at that moment busy arranging the corpse. 'That being so, I *have* to inform the King. I would suggest that your best course is to accompany me when I tell him what has happened, so that we can all three discuss what is to be done.'

'Discuss it with the King? In person?'

He had brightened up immediately. In fact his face, anywhere else but in a death chamber, would have presented a richly comic spectacle. I suspected that his position in the Royal Household was provider of placebos for chambermaids, and if he had been at the death of the King's predecessor it was as holder of the ninth slop-pail. But it was good that I now had him on my side. I turned to the attendant Bishop.

'The room where I was very graciously received in private by the King on my first visit here – is it likely to be free at the moment?'

'So far as I know . . . sir.'

'Very well. Be so good as to take Mr Nussey there, and stay on duty at the door to prevent intruders. I will go and, if it is possible, fetch the King.'

I was made to feel my want of polish: one does not 'fetch' a king. But after a moment his eyebrow was lowered and he turned and led the way. We left Mrs Hattersley in charge (looking balefully at me, to say that she'd *warned* me) and proceeded in silence down the marathon stretch of corridors and stairs, until we separated and I went back to the rooms that abutted on to the terrace. The King, the Queen and the hardier souls were still outside, and I followed them out. The King was surrounded by a little group of visitors to the castle, and the open air was encouraging him to talk even louder than usual.

'M' brother Ernest's trouble's never been women. Better if it had been. Natural. His trouble is he's the damnedest old reactionary who ever drew breath, and he thinks he can do what he likes and nobody has a right to criticise. Doesn't do these days, eh? Democratic times. Well, he'll have Hanover when I go. They don't have queens in Hanover, and it's their loss. Damn fool idea – look at the great queens we've had: Elizabeth, and that other one, Anne. We'll have another one soon, mark my words. I lived in Hanover when I was not much more than a boy. Nasty hole of a place. Send Ernest there and he'll be perfectly at home. Place is full of damned reactionaries just like himself. Suit him down to the ground. Ah, Mr Mozart.'

I had joined myself on the group and had been sending signals that passed him by.

'I wonder, Your Majesty, if I might have a private word . . .'

He nodded, with a touch of endearing self-importance.

'Ah, business, business. Just when I was enjoying m'self.' But he jogged over to me and let me lead him towards the door, back into the castle, and towards the study. Active as I am, I puffed a little in his wake, and was able to get a few words in.

'Something very extraordinary, very unfortunate has come up, sir, and we felt we couldn't act without express orders from Your Majesty,' I managed to say at last. 'Ah, here we are.' We went past the footman, his eye fixed on eternity, and I introduced him to the nervous man standing by the table and fiddling with his coat buttons. 'Mr Nussey, Your Majesty – one of the court apothecaries.'

Mr Nussey bowed exceptionally low.

'Not too much of the scraping, eh, Mr Nussey?' said the King deflatingly. 'I'm a plain man. If you can invent a cure for my asthma I'd be obliged to you, but otherwise I'm healthy enough. I'd be healthier out at sea, but it wouldn't do for m' ministers to have to come out in a bum boat every time they wanted an audience, eh?' He sat down, and graciously gestured to us to do likewise. 'Now, what is it, eh? Eh?'

I told him in a low voice and quite unemotionally the events of the last half-hour, starting with Mr Popper's exit from the Crimson Drawing Room, his death from presumed poisoning. ('That's unheard of, b'God!') and going on to the revelation that he had helped himself to the wine in other people's glasses, including the Princess Victoria's. ('But I helped the little thing to that m'self.') If there were signs that the King would have favoured a straight cover-up if it had been only Mr Popper in question, the news that it was possibly the Princess Victoria who was the intended victim altered his attitude completely. When

I had finished my exposition he sat back in his chair cogitating – slowly, but not without result. His question when it came was a cogent one.

'Who could conceivably investigate this?' I saw the point at once, but he went on, 'The local magistrates? Bow Street runners? The idea is ridiculous. They'd be so overawed by everyone here – most of them with a handle to their names, a prime minister, Royal Family – they'd be too busy scraping and minding their Ps and Qs to get to the bottom of anything. I tell you what they'd do, Mr Mozart: they'd fix on one of you theatre people, because they wouldn't have to scrape to them. Probably be you, eh? Eh?'

'Probably, Your Majesty. Mr Popper himself was accustomed to blame me for pretty much everything that went wrong. The fact that I am a foreigner would probably convince any normal investigator that I was guilty.'

'Foreigner? Nonsense. You're a true blue Englishman, I can see that.' Ugh. 'But we've got to do better than that. Got to get to the bottom of it and *stop it*. Lovely little girl – hope of the nation and all that. If it's a feller we'll send him into a room with a revolver. If it's a woman – don't know what we'll do. Pity we don't have nunneries. Very useful things, nunneries, if you had a wrong-'un to put away . . . If the Duchess gets wind of this she'll take the Princess away quick as lightning.'

'Would that be such a bad thing, Your Majesty?'

He shook his head.

'Then we might never get to the bottom of the thing. Think of it: all the people who came with her would be out of reach of questioning.'

'But surely the people from Kensington Palace would not wait till they came to Windsor Castle before trying to kill her? They'd have much better opportunities at home.'

'But if they tried to kill her at home they'd be the first to be suspected. Here they'd be the last.' The King saw the expression on my face, and immediately responded – quietly, without trace of having taken offence. 'Ha, Mr Mozart! So you've put me down as a silly old buffer who hasn't an idea in his head, have you? You're not the only one. Well, I may ramble on a bit and say things I shouldn't, but I can think things through if

I have to. I tell you what, a modern king doesn't have to be too clever, or he'll find his position intolerable – all power in theory, none in practice, that's what he has. But he shouldn't be too stupid either, or he'll find the politicians walking over him. And I tell you, Mr Mozart, I may not be a great brain, but I am not stupid.'

I hastily began, 'I assure you, Your Majesty—'

He waved his hand.

'Pooh, pooh! I'm not offended. You're not a scraper, Mr Mozart. That's why I took to you at once. You speak your mind, or let it show on your face. Well, now you know I can think, let me think this through. Some kind of poison, you say—'

'Possibly digitalis, Your Majesty,' put in Mr Nussey, the first words he had dared say since the discussion began. King William nodded, as if we were discussing different blends of tea.

'So, since no one could have known I was going to press the Princess to have a glass of wine, it must have been put in – if it *was* her glass – between my handing it to her and the silly fool drinking it down ... The thing is: who? Now, you'll do the investigation, of course Mr Mozart.'

'But, Your Majesty—!'

He stopped my protests with a gesture.

'Obvious person. Long history of services. Kept m'brother Ernest out of the newspapers and the courts for once in his life – not that he deserved it, damn' fool that he is, or thanked you for it either, knowing him. Then there was that business at the Queen's Theatre.'

'But Your Majesty, I thought—'

'That it was all hushed up? So it was. But Lady Hertford told m'brother the King – last bid to keep her hold on him. Didn't work. But he told me years later. Nice work. Very loyal. So what we do is: Mr – er – Nussey signs the certificate.' He turned in his direction. 'Very grateful to you. Won't forget it. Call you in if the other chappies are sick. Just tell people there's been a sudden unfortunate death from – from what? Eh?'

'Heart, Your Majesty.'

'Heart. Safe that. Always heart at the end, eh? I'll set a footman the particular task of guarding the Princess Victoria.

And you, Mr Mozart, have the rest of the Princess's visit to find out who wishes her harm.'

Without telling anybody that any harm has been intended her, or that anyone has died an unnatural death. King William had the regal habit of demanding the impossible and assuming it would be done for him. In the most gracious manner, of course.

NINE
Past and Present

I found it very difficult to go back and mingle with the assembled company as if nothing had happened. The King didn't find it difficult at all. He bustled in on his guests and within minutes I heard him telling details of the indiscretions of one of the old Queen's ladies-in-waiting to a couple I was convinced were the lady in question's daughter and son-in-law. A technique was evolving for dealing with the King's spectacular *faux pas*. You kept quiet while they were being committed and got together with other victims later to compare notes. Though affection for the new King was undimmed, there was a feeling that for one whose life had been a series of more or less comic indiscretions, he had an unconscionable relish for the follies of others.

The company had thinned out a little: the actors had gone back to London, and I looked in vain for the scamp who had attached himself to the Princess Sophia. I was filled with an uneasy sense of needing to make a start, without any idea of how to proceed. Really the King had presented me with an impossible task. Seeing that the Duchess of Kent was leafing through fashionable journals by the fireside I decided to begin my investigations with her: she had been, after all, on the alert about the well-being of her daughter even before the events of the afternoon. Those events should be clear in her mind. She greeted my approach with every appearance of pleasure.

'Mr Mozart! You have been talking to the King?'

'I have, Ma'am,' I said, bowing, and accepting the seat she gestured to. 'The King takes a serious view of the ... disturbance this afternoon.'

'I vould hope he does!' said the Duchess, understandably.

'Of course. And he has taken various measures as a consequence. A footman will, unobtrusively, always be close to the Princess Victoria for the rest of her stay here, and a letter has been sent to the Duke of Cumberland threatening him with arrest if he comes within the vicinity of the castle again during her visit.'

The Duchess nodded, but not too happily.

'I am sadly confused as to vether I should stay on. I shall never be anything but extremely uneasy here. There is bad blood in that family, Mr Mozart.'

'There is certainly something about the Duke of Cumberland that makes one uneasy,' I admitted.

'And you have cause to know, Mr Mozart,' she said graciously.

'I have cause to know,' I agreed. 'It is not something I can speak about.'

'I respect your discretion. There have, however, been rumours in the family . . . Of course it may be that Sir John is right: in such a public place no harm vould be attempted. And the fact that the Duke is the most hated man in England may also be a sort of protection. But then he is *mad*! Who but a madman vould do what he did today?'

'Who indeed?' I echoed. Though I had reason to believe that the Duke was in fact most unpleasantly sane. I added, 'I think I must have had a presentiment of what he was going to do.'

'*Really?*' said the Duchess, as interested in such superstitious nonsense as any washerwoman or any actor would be.

'Yes,' I said, simulating a rapt recall of the situation. 'I remember turning away from the company just before the first shot rang out and noting with particular sharpness what was happening around the Princess. Of course I regard her – if I may say so without presumption – in the light of a charge.'

'And I am very glad that you do, and very grateful for your promptness ven you heard the shots.'

'Nothing but my duty – and, at my age, nothing like so fast as Your Royal Highness.' We gave rather comic little bows at each other, and then I resumed. 'No, I remember so vividly that the Princess had been talking to the Duke of Wellington – a delightful picture they made together! The Duke then went off to talk to you: he joined the group you made with Lord Grey and Lord Melbourne.'

'He came vith empty compliments about Victoria,' said the Duchess sourly. The Hero of Waterloo cut no ice with her, and she did not even seem pleased with compliments to her daughter.

'And the Princess was then joined by the King and Queen, and he pressed her to take a glass of wine.'

'Have you ever heard such foolishness?' asked the Duchess indignantly. 'I should have gone over then.'

'She sipped it, and he turned away. I have it there on my mind, like a posed picture – a formal painting by Sir Thomas Lawrence, perhaps. The Queen was still beside the Princess when the shots rang out. The figures around the table and the sofa are much more blurred, however.'

'George FitzClarence was there,' the Duchess said promptly. 'I know *that* because if he had tried to talk to Victoria I vould have gone over at once.'

'Was he with anyone, or on his own?'

'He vas talking to . . . oh dear, who vas it? His vife is not here: she is in an interesting condition, as the FitzClarences alvays seem to be. Trying to make up in number vot they lack in legitimacy . . . I think it vas Lady Courtney, one of the Queen's ladies-in-waiting. The FitzClarences alvays hang around the Queen, you notice, as if they're trying to claim her as their mother.'

'And yet they don't always seem properly respectful of her,' I pointed out.

'There you are, you see: divided, confused, mad!'

'I seem to remember that some of the theatre people were close by too.'

'That little man like a turkey-cock. The manager, I believe? And young George Cambridge vas making himself ridiculous vith that actress – *how* such things run in the family! But I can't remember vether they vere close or not.'

The Duchess was now claimed by the Queen, and I was glad because if we had gone on with the conversation much longer she would surely have wanted to know why I was so interested in who was near the Princess. I had not got very far, but it did occur to me that the person to ask might be the Princess herself. I slipped up to my room, where a fire had been lit (it was a room not totally inconspicuous and removed from the 'good' society staying at the castle – very different treatment from my last experience of staying with royalty), and at the little desk-cum-toilet table I penned the following note:

> Let us play a game – a memory game. Let us imagine that the recent shots were real shots, intended to harm, and the affair is being investigated by magistrates. They ask you where you were, who you were talking to, and who was around you. How much do you remember? What would be your reply?
>
> Nemo

I was not at all sure, to tell the truth, that the Princess would be deceived by the pretence of this being a game. She was not easily deceived. I was sure, though, that she would be delighted by the business of passing surreptitious notes.

My opportunity occurred soon after I returned to the general company. The Duchess of Kent had decreed that the Princess was not to dine with her elders for a second night running ('Too much excitement'), and the King in his kindly way was looking for some means of compensating her and giving her prominence, for all his guests were intensely interested in her, and he had not the slightest feeling of jealousy. His choice of method was not entirely happy. He was insisting to her that she play for the assembled company. The Princess stood out for a while, then seeing me approach she giggled and gave in. When the chatter and din had been stilled by footmen the King stood by the piano.

'I don't know if you know, but m'niece is a fine little pianist. She's very reluctant, but she's said she'll play one little piece for us. While I'm on the subject of music, we've had some fine musicians playing here at Windsor – this new chap Mendelssohn only last year – but I venture to say her teacher—' he caught the eye of the Queen – 'but I mustn't go on – m'niece.'

His taking notice of the Queen for once suggested to me that he had realised that it was probably better not to give me undue prominence at the moment. Pity – a royal endorsement as the greatest living musician in Europe would have made a nice change, and could have been relayed to the newspapers to impress my creditors. Ah well. I emerged from rummaging through the available music to find that the Princess was standing, diminutive, in front of the piano stool and was about to say something.

'The King is very kind,' she announced in her bell-like tones which made such a change from Hanoverian gruffness, 'but I want to say that I don't play well at all, and it won't be very pleasant having to listen. But you must know that it's not at all Mr Mozart's fault, because in fact he's only given me three lessons, and even he can't work miracles in that time.'

She sat down amid laughter, and as people were looking at each other and smiling indulgently I slipped the note into her hand, and as she arranged her music with her left hand, with her right she popped the note into the neck of her dress.

She played the inevitable Clementi and – stimulated, perhaps, by the little spurt of excitement at receiving the note – managed it better than she ever had before, with quite a show of brilliance from time to time. I saw Sir John Conroy gazing at her with a pride that seemed to announce itself as paternal. Foolish man – just the way to arouse enmities in the circle in which he was mixing. The over-mighty subject was something we had all had quite enough of in the last reign, with the King's succession of rapacious mistresses. The applause at the end was genuine, and it was with no show of regret that the Princess allowed herself to be packed off upstairs to join the other children in a nursery supper, while we indulged in or endured another formal dinner.

I was placed at table among decidedly better company than I had had the day before, though whether this was by order of the King or due to an error on the part of his household I never found out. Of course 'good' company, in that sense, can have its drawbacks. On one side of me was Lord Howe, the Queen's Chamberlain whom I've mentioned before – an unpleasant, chilly figure with reactionary opinions. He was so incensed at finding himself sitting next to a common fiddler that he spoke no word to me at all, and was forced to put up some pretence of conversation with Earl Grey on the other side of him – a man whom he obviously regarded as the Robespierre of current British politics. Opposite him was the King's son-in-law the Earl of Erroll – a boisterous, headstrong Whig whom he found it equally difficult to be polite to, so there was usually a pool of silence and ill-will on my right.

I was luckier on my left hand, where I had the Countess of Erroll. I must not bore you with how lovely her mother Mrs Jordan was. Nothing is more tedious than old men going on about the charms of actresses of their younger days. But – oh! – this woman did remind me of her, with her enchanting laugh, her beauty, with a touch of the elfin and a touch of the hoyden, and the gift – just like her mother's – of making you think you are the most interesting and fascinating man in the world.

Inevitably we started talking about the Duke of Cumberland's escapade that afternoon. Everyone else was talking about it, so how could we avoid it?

'Of course he *hates* Papa, since he opposed him over Catholic Emancipation,' she said.

'I remember,' I said truthfully, that measure having interested me more than most of the futile Acts passed by Parliament since it concerned my co-religionists. 'What was it your father called his brother's opposition to the Bill?'

'"Factious and infamous". He'd got up the description beforehand – that's not his usual sort of language at all.' She put back her head and laughed. 'Usually it smacks of the quarterdeck, as everyone knows. But that was the sort of formal language the Duke of Cumberland understands. He's very vocal on the need to be loyal to Established Authority, but in practice he is only loyal if he agrees with the Established Authority.'

'There are many such,' I said.

'Today was an act of defiance of my father. He was cocking a snook at the new régime. He could bully the old King, but he can't this one. It's very unpleasant because Papa and my mother were very kind to the Duke's son.' She saw my surprise and added, with a charming smile, 'His natural son. We had quite a collection of children in a state of nature at Bushey.'

'It must have been a good childhood.'

'It was. Mama was always in the family way, but it never seemed to make any difference – it was like a stage role she could do without thinking any time a manager asked her to. She and my father doted on children, and just wanted us to have a carefree and happy time as we grew up. They knew things would become difficult later on. I think Papa had through us the childhood he had never had when young.'

'So it never made any difference that you were . . . natural children?'

She thought.

'Not when we were very young. I remember wondering why everyone always talked very respectfully of Grandmama Queen and Grandpapa King, but we never actually *saw* them. I decided they must live a long, long way away. I never ever met, never was received by, either of them.'

'When did you really understand?'

'When I was about ten, Mama gradually . . . disappeared. Wasn't there. I was at a stage – I think we all went through it – of having fantasies that Papa and Mama had really been married, that we would be found to be little princes and princesses. I wasn't of an age to understand the Royal Marriages Act. And then, suddenly, the ground was taken away from under me. Mama was no longer *there*, but we knew she was still alive – we visited her from time to time, and she tried to explain what had happened. But our governess was in effect our mother, and there was talk of Papa marrying – not *again*, but marrying. I was not a little princess, and we were just a brood of natural children who were generally something of an embarrassment.'

'And your mother died alone in France.'

There was a moment's silence. She shot me a look.

'You knew my mother, didn't you?'

I felt greatly daring, speaking out.

'Of course. I was working in the theatre, and she was the greatest comic actress of the time. The greatest I have ever seen. To meet she was one of the most delightful women I have ever known. To think of her end is almost unbearable.'

'Yes.' We were silent for a moment. 'I was very young, you know, Mr Mozart. Only fifteen. One is not mistress of oneself at fifteen.'

'Lady Erroll, I am not accusing you—'

'But people do. People who knew and loved her. And perhaps they are right. When she and my father separated I suppose unconsciously we children knew that our future had to be with Papa. If you like, we knew which side our bread was buttered. My sister Sophia was rather cruel, I'm afraid. She was just entering the world, and was at an age when you *are* ruthless, are desperate to preserve what you've got, and get more. George was better – but George may have had his reasons ... I think we were all more or less selfish, and more or less ruthless, as children and young men and women usually are.'

'And now you have another mother, who seems a very good one, in a different way.'

She looked down the table to where the Queen sat, placid and dowdy as usual.

'Oh yes. Too good for us. We bully her. William, my husband bullies her because her opinions are so dyed-in-the-wool. She seems to have been born old, with old opinions ... My mother was Papa's young wife. My stepmother is his *old* wife, even though she's half his age. Oh dear, I do hope Papa is not going to speak again.'

But he was merely getting up to bow to the Queen as she led the ladies from the Waterloo Chamber. Barbarous habit. I dislike port because I associate it with all-male company. I endured it for as short a time as was decent, frozen by Lord Howe on my right and subject to good-humoured banter from Lord Erroll opposite, and then escaped. Before rejoining the ladies I decided to go up to my room, to adjust my *toilette* after the exigencies of a long, royal meal (I am by some accounted vain of my appearance, though I merely have a proper respect for social appearances and the requirements of the ladies). When I got to my chamber I was surprised to find a note on my little table, and could not think who it was from. Even the name on it, 'Mr Mosart' did not give it away (misspelling, ignorance and childish handwriting being endemic among the upper classes). When I opened the note I could not forebear chuckling.

At the time of the schocking events this after noon I was standing near to the fireplace. The Queen was beside me conversing grashously, and the King was just departing, having given me a glass of clarret which I did not want and meerly pretended to drink. Near me was George FitzClarence who is one of the *most handsomest* men I have ever seen though not I think a happy one, and he was talking to the Queen's ladie in waiting. There were other people around, but you forget Mr Mosart that I have not been in Society and *know* nobody. When the first shot rang out (he should be consined to a dunjon for the rest of his life, the horrible beast!) Mama ran over and you more sloly, Mama stood in front of me, and then we both sank to the flore. After a few shots we realized there was no danger and we both got up and went causously to the window and watched the ridickulous specktacle my uncle was making of himself.

Have I not done well? It was one of the most schockingly exciting things that ever happened to me, so I should remember.

Your freind and Princess

V.

I snuffed the candle and stood there smiling. I folded the note and put it in an inside pocket. This note from the Princess Victoria should be willed to my children or grandchildren. It would be a family treasure that could be turned into real treasure in the sort of emergency to which everyone in the musical profession – even a humble teacher in a girls' school – from time to time falls victim. Then I thought again. There must be no danger of anyone, but expecially her mother or Sir John, finding out about our agreement, and our special relationship. Regretfully I took the note from my pocket and consigned it to the ashes of the fire.

TEN
Families

When I went down to rejoin the fine company they were reviving from a post-prandial somnolence and becoming quite lively. Lord Melbourne, in particular, was surrounded by younger ladies, a condition that seemed to please him mightily: he was entertaining them with stories that periodically aroused gales of soprano laughter. I was looking around me to choose who next to attach myself to when the choice was made for me. I felt a presence at my shoulder.

'Mr Mozart—'

'Ah, Sir John.'

'Might I have a word in your ear – in private?'

I surveyed the scene and nodded towards a dim and unoccupied corner of the Crimson Drawing Room where we were. Sir John Conroy nodded, and I followed his imposing military back through the laughing, drinking crowd until we gained the relative peace and privacy of the corner. He cleared his throat.

'Mr Mozart, I think we have the same objectives as far as the Princess Victoria's future is concerned.'

Up to a point, Sir John, I thought. But I nodded. He was a man it was advisable to agree with.

'I'm sure we do, Sir John. It is hardly my business, of course – ' he gestured, as if to dismiss my disclaimer – 'but I would certainly hope to see, and soon, the Princess properly supported by the Country she will one day rule over, and accorded all the state due to her position. With respect, I feel that the Duchess's desire to keep her far from the corruptions and contaminations of Society, though admirable in itself, will hardly prove practical in the long run. It would be unfortunate if the Princess suddenly became Queen of a country she knew little of, and a leader of Society which she had never been into.'

Sir John nodded.

'Moderation in all things, I agree. But as we told you we – that is, the Duchess has plans for progresses around the country, where the Princess would stay in the best houses. That will introduce her into Society, *selected* parts of Society.' He paused and looked at me. I didn't argue. 'On the subject of the Princess's financial position—'

'Yes?'

He leaned forward.

'I think I may tell you that I have had talks since we arrived, and the position may well be altered substantially for the better. There are one or two conditions attached to the offer which the Duchess would not accept, but which I am sure, through negotiations, we can get rid of.'

Ah ha! I thought. They're using the bait of increased money to try and loosen his hold on the purse strings, as I suggested. And he's resisting. He hasn't yet realised, I suspect, what he is up against.

'That is most satisfactory,' I said.

'It is very important, therefore, that nothing is done, nothing *happens*, to make the Duchess fly the castle, with the Princess. She is, you will have noticed, very much inclined to do just that, in spite of the better position that is in prospect for her.'

'It would be unfortunate, in the circumstances,' I agreed.

'Very unfortunate indeed ... You seem, Mr Mozart, to be close to the King.'

He fixed me with the sort of eye a commander on the field of battle uses on a junior officer who has failed in his duty. I was ready for him.

'I have in the past done some service to the King's family,' I said, an expression of unusual modesty on my face.

'Ah yes, I have heard rumours,' he said suavely. 'The matter of the Duke of Cumberland and—'

'I think we should say no more.' I said it as a rebuke, though I don't think Sir John recognised it as such. He was not easily put down. 'I should add, though, that, given the choice, the

Duke is *not* the member of the family I would have chosen to perform a service for.'

'I'm glad to hear it.'

'And there is in fact another service to the King's family which is not generally known – ' my expression grew quite seraphically modest – 'and of which I certainly cannot speak.'

'Really?' His tongue flicked over his lips.

'I *cannot* speak of it, even though most of the principals in the matter are dead.'

He hid his disappointment.

'Your discretion does you credit, Mr Mozart,' he said insincerely, 'and explains why the King has such confidence in you. But it is the fact of your known services to the family, Mr Mozart, that made the Duchess a little uneasy earlier, when you seemed to be exceptionally interested in who was near the Princess at the time of the . . . shooting incident.'

Light dawned. Never underestimate people. Especially women. Luckily by now I had my explanation ready.

'She need not be uneasy. Quite the reverse. The King is merely being especially cautious.'

'Oh?'

'Yes. He is quite sure that the incident you refer to is merely one of his brother's foolish and offensive pranks. There have of course been others.'

'Indeed.'

'This one was clearly intended to "cock a snook" at himself and his new dignity as King. He has, as you know, refused to invite his brother to this gathering at Windsor at your – at the Duchess's insistence.'

'Yes – but I don't yet follow you, Mr Mozart.'

'The King just wants to be *doubly* certain that there might not have been the aim of distracting attention while someone else attempted to harm the Princess – an aim which was foiled by the Duchess's prompt action in going to her side.'

'Ah, I see!' His face lit up. 'I must say I would not have thought that the King—'

'Never underestimate people,' I said virtuously. He smiled his fat-cat smile, and I decided this was a lesson he was too self-satisfied to learn.

'That is very satisfactory, at any rate. I think I will give the explanation to the Duchess in toned-down, more general terms, so as not to agitate her.' He spoke of her as if he were her proprietor – or as if she were a pampered lap-dog and he her owner. 'I think it would be fair to say, would it not, that the King is very keen to accord the Princess the position which her status as Heiress Presumptive demands?'

To be consulted on a king's thoughts!

'Most certainly,' I assured him solemnly. 'And hopeful of getting to know the Princess better, though I have suggested that he and the Queen should go slowly on that matter.'

'Slowly. That's right, Mr Mozart. Very slowly indeed.'

He smiled again that smile of self-love, and led the way back to the company, his whole being suggesting that he had found the conversation most satisfactory. I was once again possessed of the conviction that he was not honest, and not intelligent. The latter was easily provable: what intelligent man would so antagonise the child on whom his future and his fortunes depended? His dishonesty was more difficult to prove. And I had to remind myself that it was his relationship with the Duchess of Kent that was the reason why I had become so involved with the household and its affairs. That was the most difficult of all to investigate.

I was disturbed from my reverie by a middle-aged lady with the face of an amiable cart-horse who had come up close to me and was beckoning. I pulled myself together and followed her. As we went towards the door she whispered 'The Queen'. We slipped through the door, and casting another surreptitious look at the long oval of her face I remembered where I had seen her: she was one of Queen Adelaide's ladies-in-waiting – Lady Courtney, I thought. We slipped down the length of St George's Hall – if one can slip down so grand a chamber – and eventually we came to one of the splendid and ornate rooms devoted to the use of the nation's queens over the centuries. It was a high, gilded chamber, with a grand painted ceiling of gods in various stages of undress, splendid tapestries and formal family portraits from the time of Charles II. In the midst of all this grandeur, not so much dwarfed as crushed by it, sat our plain, nice, ordinary little Queen. As we approached her she assumed an expression of welcome, mixed with one of roguishness, as if it was quite an adventure to summon a man to talk to her.

'Ah, Mr Mozart, so good of you to come to talk to me.'

It was a nice voice – gentle and musical. It certainly contrasted with her husband's guttural barks.

'Oh, Your Majesty, a queen's summons—'

'Oh!' she said, dismissively, 'Don't bother with that stuff! I am such a new queen, and who knows how long I will be Queen at all.'

'His Majesty looks extraordinarily fit for his age.'

Her expression became one of sad foreboding.

'Oh, I was not meaning the King's health, I was talking about the revolutionary spirit abroad. The French King has been chased out of his country, and the Dutch King has been chased out of Belgium. In France they have a Citizen King. What nonsense! How can you have a Citizen King?

I forebore to say that in this country we seemed to have got a Citizen King too, and without the bother of a revolution. I stood there trying to look sympathetic without compromising my democratic principles. She went on, 'What a world! Who knows who will be next? The rabble are crying "Reform" here. Well – if I lose my head I will not be as beautiful as the French Queen who lost hers, but I will try to be as brave!'

I had to repress a smile.

'The British often ridicule their Royal Family, Ma'am, and on occasion they even throw things, but it is a long time since they executed a king or queen. I cannot see them starting again in the nineteenth century.'

Her eyes widened.

'But the mob – it is trying its strength . . . But let us not talk about that.'

I bowed, wondering what we would talk about. She gestured me to a capacious chair, on which I perched, feeling myself very small (I am not a large man), and wondering what manner of man the chair could have been made to contain. Perhaps only the late King could really have filled it.

'Mr Mozart, the King trusts you.'

'I am greatly honoured by his good opinion, Ma'am.'

95

'You have already had several conferences together since you arrived at the castle.'

I dipped my head.

'We have indeed talked more than once.'

'Mr Mozart, the King always talks any domestic matters over with me, anything connected with the family.' She hesitated and I nodded encouragingly. 'But matters of state he does not discuss, does not think women are capable of understanding. He is old-fashioned – which is what I prefer. Old fashion is good fashion. However . . . I wonder if you can tell me, Mr Mozart, if it is a matter of state he has been talking over with you?'

I shook my head vigorously. I wanted no more connection with any matter of state.

'Oh, Your Majesy, I have nothing to do with matters of state, loathe politics of any kind' (not quite true, though I certainly distrust politicians). 'If the King has not talked the matter over with you I am sure it is because he doesn't want to alarm you, or because he has not had the opportunity, with so many people at the castle at the moment.'

'Then it is a matter of family?'

'Naturally the incident this afternoon with the Duke of Cumberland—'

'Ah! Then it is not his children, but his brother?'

That, I thought, was an interesting assumption of hers. I tried to soothe her.

'The King was naturally concerned after such a . . . display.'

'Alas, poor Ernest,' said the Queen sorrowfully. Her face was naturally tuned in to sorrow. 'He has excellent principles – strong, true, well-tried principles. But his behaviour! It is atrocious!' She shook her head. 'I am afraid he gives good Conservative principles a bad name.'

I was pleased to think he probably did.

'That is decidedly so, Your Majesty. And the Royal Family as well, unless he is kept in check.'

'And where do *you* come in, Mr Mozart?'

'I . . . have had experience with the Duke in the past, Ma'am. I *know* him extremely well.'

'Of course! I have heard whispers.'

96

'And I am very much concerned with my pupil, the Princess Victoria. That is where the King's worry lies.' I pulled out my lie again. 'Probably it was only a madcap prank that we saw earlier, but the King was concerned by the possibility that it might have been designed to distract attention from something else, something more serious.'

'I see,' said the Queen thoughtfully. She smiled a watery smile. 'He is very wise, William. People do not understand how wise he is. They underestimate him. People who try to take advantage are in for a shock.'

'Lady Erroll was saying at table what an excellent father he was to her and her brothers and sisters.'

The Queen displayed some agitation.

'When I talk about taking advantage I do not mean his children. We are a heppy family, very heppy. The boys of course are not heppy about their position. It is difficult for them. George in particular, as the eldest. George feels it very much. But I was thinking of . . . others.'

I nodded and waited, but nothing came.

'I was noticing today, during the performance of my little play,' I murmured, to keep the conversation going, 'and then again later on—'

'Yes?'

'I noticed a man. A man who looked . . . somewhat out of place here. He was sitting during the performance with the Princess Sophia, or at least next to her. And later they were walking in the grounds when . . .'

I suddenly realised that the lady-in-waiting, behind the sofa, was vigorously shaking her head. It was too late. The Queen had reddened with embarrassment.

'Ah! What shall I say? You should ask the King. Or perhaps Princess Sophia. What do you think, Courtney? No, perhaps not the Princess. Though . . . At any rate I cannot be the one who talks about him.'

I stood up.

'I am afraid I have distressed Your Majesty.'

'No, no, Mr Mozart – not at all. But dear Sophia – so graceful, so charming, so much fun.' She said it wistfully, as if she would have given anything to be a bit of fun herself. 'I would not want

97

her to be distressed, you understand? Ask the King. It is not important.'

At a nod from the lady-in-waiting I bowed myself out, wondering why, if it was not a matter of importance, the good lady had become so agitated. And as I walked through the ornate spaces of the castle I thought over the new Queen's conversation and reactions and could only come to the conclusion that she was suppressing anxieties about the King's natural children, and overlaying them with concern about his being taken advantage of by someone else. The most natural candidate would surely be the Duchess of Kent – of whom the Queen might naturally feel somewhat jealous, since she was the mother of the heir – had provided an heir to the throne where she had failed. In view of the suspicions about her and Sir John, her jealousy could be augmented by moral disapproval.

Back in the Drawing Rooms the company had thinned out. The Duchess and her party were certainly among those who had gone to their (separate, I had no doubt) beds, and so were many more. The King however still had an audience for whatever he wanted to say, as Kings do, and it was quite difficult to get him on his own. I talked for a time to Lord Melbourne, who is agreeable for a politician, and easy with all ranks and callings. He was utterly delighted by my pupil, her charm and her prospects.

'*What* a delightful child,' he said enthusiastically. 'How you must enjoy giving her lessons.'

'I have seldom had a pupil I've had more pleasure from,' I said truthfully. 'Though the pleasure is seldom musical.'

'Don't be an old sourpuss, Mr Mozart. What a queen she will make, eh?'

'I don't suppose I will be around to see it, but it should certainly be interesting.'

His face lit up and became almost roguish.

'Interesting? It will be amusing. It will be the jolliest court since Charles II.' His face fell. 'But there – I don't suppose I'll be around to see it either.'

'Will you excuse me, My Lord?'

The King's actions had caught my eye. He had an endearing habit of going over to the waiters when he wanted a drink, rather than summoning them. It enabled him to change the group he was talking to, to share himself around, a trait that was most appreciated. This time I intercepted him.

'Your Majesty.'

'Ah, Mr Mozart.' He turned to me most agreeably. 'How are you going, eh? Things becoming a little clearer?'

'Not a great deal, sir. But I am trying to fill in details. There was something the Queen said I ought to ask you about.'

'Oh?' he said cagily.

'The man who sat beside the Princess Sophia at the play, the one she was later walking with in the gardens – who is he?'

He drew his finger along under his nose, and wiped it on his breeches. It seemed like a ruse to avoid answering immediately.

'Ah! What do you want to know that for?'

'It's one of the details I need to fill in, sir.'

He got truculent.

'Don't see why. He was in the garden. Nowhere near the Princess.'

'I nevertheless need to know what is going on, Your Majesty – everything that is going on. I could ask the Princess—'

'And she would tell you. Oh, very well. I thought it would give her pleasure, inviting him. Hasn't had a great deal of pleasure in her life, poor Sophy. Damned awful life, to tell you the truth. And I do like to bring people together after misunderstandings. I knew the Duchess wouldn't know who he was, so she couldn't make any trouble. I thought if they could meet again, they could talk, get to know each other better.'

He bumbled into silence.

'And he is?'

'He's her son, Mr Mozart. I thought everyone knew she'd had a son.'

ELEVEN

Out of the Mouths of Drunkards

I stood for a few seconds in shocked silence. I was remembering something the Princess Victoria had said during our first lesson. When we'd talked about the pressures on princes that led to liaisons rather than marriages, natural rather than legal children, she had said, 'And not just princes.' Her aunt's case was obviously what she'd been thinking of (and it was a safe bet that her knowledge of the matter had been gained from below-stairs rather than above, and would have been an unpleasant surprise to her mother, Sir John, and Lehzen). And dredging still further back in my memory I recalled that there had been stories – so long ago I had little idea when – of the Princess giving birth to a son at Weymouth. Eventually I realised I had to say something.

'So Your Majesty asked this young man – whatever his name is—'

'Tom Garth.'

'—Tom Garth, so that he and his mother could get to know each other better.'

'That's right,' said the King, with a sort of nervous complacency, as if he had convinced himself he had done the right thing, but was slightly nervous that he had done a very foolish one. 'Met him in the street. Seemed a nice enough fellow. Very anxious to get to know his mother better. Natural, ah?'

I began to see the point of kings *not* pottering around the streets chatting to their subjects.

'Your Majesty didn't ask any other children?' I asked, hardly able to keep the irony out of my voice. 'There was mention at dinner of a natural son of the Duke of Cumberland.'

100

His face fell at once.

'Dead. Poor FitzErnest. We did our best for him, Dora and I. Never came to anything.'

'And the Princess and her son had met before?'

'Oh yes. But not often. Awkward, y'know.'

Another memory, much more recent, stirred in my mind.

'Wasn't there talk, a year or two ago, of some attempt to blackmail the Princess Sophia?'

The King's nervousness increased, but he dismissed the matter with a wave.

'All a misunderstanding. He told me all about it. The poor lad had confided the story of his background to an unscrupulous fellow who took advantage of it without his knowing. Silly matter, all blown up. I'm sure he and his mother will have sorted it all out today. Clears the air, eh?'

Muddies the water more like, I thought. This was just the sort of good-hearted but dangerous gesture that should *not* have been made when the Duchess of Kent and her daughter were on a visit that was likely to be at best ticklish. But I took one look at him, at his naive air of wanting approval, of willing me to share his desire to think well of people, and I merely said, 'I'm sure there's no harm done, Your Majesty,' and bowed my withdrawal.

I was going to have to revise my opinion of the King yet again. Yes, he was sharper than people thought, more able to think things through. But there was an exception: not where his own family were concerned. That applied most forcefully to his wife and his natural brood, of course. But it also applied to other family members he was fond of – the Princess Victoria, his sisters. All the children of George III and Queen Charlotte had had pretty grim childhoods. The girls had had grim womanhoods as well. The instinct to make it up to them had apparently existed even in George IV's selfish bosom. It clearly was vigorously alive in King William's more generous one.

But if the King had no eye for an obvious scamp, what chance was there of his recognising a more subtle one?

I was standing, as it happened, in the shadow of a large footman who was immobile but ready to minister condescendingly to the thinning throng. Most had had more than enough, but there were always some for whom more than enough is insufficient. As I stood there, thoughtful, there approached two of our most eminent statesmen, on their way out of the assembly and towards their bedrooms. They were making no effort to keep their voices down, so I felt it no shame to listen to what they were saying. The two were Lord Melbourne and the Duke of Wellington, talking with the surface amiability which concealed deep-rooted political antagonism.

'I've just had the most extraordinary conversation with FitzClarence,' said Lord Melbourne.

'I'm not surprised,' said the Duke, gloomily. 'He's getting out of hand.'

'Worse than that, I'd have said.'

'Mad?'

'On the verge of, or so it seemed to me. The King is going to have to put his foot down.'

The Duke scratched his chin.

'The King is sterling and loyal – you'll find that if you ever come in. But put his foot down with his own family? I would say it's out of the question.'

And they disappeared through the door towards the staircase. They had unwittingly confirmed the conclusions I had just come to. I was about to seek my bed too, with more than enough already to think over, when out of the corner of my eye I caught sight of a figure lurching towards the door that led to the staircase down to the terrace and the gardens. It was a tall, saturnine figure, well-set-up, but in a terrible state. I couldn't see his face, but I felt sure it was George FitzClarence.

I took a glass of claret from one of the attendant sneerers, dallied for a minute or two, then followed him.

It took some time for my eyes to accustom themselves to the gloom. There were little shreds of light from the castle, otherwise only a harvest moon to lessen the pitch blackness. As I stood there getting my bearings I heard a retching sound from the far parapet looking over into the great park. I held myself back once more: no man likes to be interrupted in his drunken vomiting. After a tactful interval, and when the sounds had stopped, I began picking my way along the geometrical paths which that very afternoon had witnessed the Duke of

Cumberland's remarkable feat of horsemanship. When I finally arrived in the vicinity of the figure which was hardly more than a shape, it was standing against the parapet, glass in hand, staring into the still greater darkness of the park.

'Good to get some fresh air,' I said inanely. He was not in a condition to object to the banality of the remark, or question why a complete stranger should approach him on a pitch-black terrace at the end of a long day.

'Fresh air, peash and quiet,' he said thickly. 'Peash from all those dishgushting hypocrites in there. I know the value of their politenesh. I know how long it will lasht.'

'Courts do seem to produce hypocrisy,' I agreed conversationally. 'I suppose it's natural really. The favour of the monarch is valuable in any number of ways. It's lucky for us that your father has kept away from courts for most of his life. His coming to the throne has opened a few doors and windows.'

'Shtill full of dishgushting hypocrites,' he said aggressively. He turned around and peered at me. 'Who are you? Are you one of the theatre people?'

'Wolfgang Gottlieb Mozart,' I said, bowing without being quite sure why I should bow.

'Used to see a lot of theatre people,' he said, his voice quieter. 'When I was a child.'

'I suppose you would have.' There was a moment's silence, as he seemed to be groping among his memories.

'Did shoo know my mother?'

That I could respond to unreservedly.

'I did indeed, though not as well as I would have liked. We didn't work for the same companies – in fact there was rivalry between the two companies. But I admired her enormously – as a woman as well as an actress. She was a remarkable person.'

'She was a lovely person. The besht woman I've known in my whole life. Worth a thousand of – ' I think he had been about to mention the new Queen, but he had just enough sense to amend it to '– any woman in there.'

'She was, she was. And not just generous and charming, but wonderfully gifted.'

'Wonderfully gifted,' he repeated. Then he added, 'And rottenly treated.'

I left a silence. He was clearly not referring to her treatment by theatrical managements or the British public, and I did not care to abuse the King while I was his guest in his castle.

'She loved shildren,' he said into the darkness. 'She was always pregnant, and she never complained, never said there were too many.'

'Your father the King seems to love children too,' I put in. 'He knows how to talk to them.'

'Bit of a child himself in shome ways,' he said brutally. 'Doeshn't shee through people. Doeshn't shee he's shurrounding himshelf with . . .' he searched for a word, but could only come up with the old one: 'hypocrites.' Then he found a new one: 'flatterers. People who are only out for what they can get. Instead of relying on people he can trusht. Wouldn't you expect a man to rely on his own children? On his shon?'

'I'm sure he does rely on you greatly.'

He leaned forward and began speaking more controlledly, more intensely.

'Then he's a funny way of showing it. Lets *that woman* walk all over him. Lets her treat his children like dirt.'

'That woman?' I asked, thinking I knew the answer.

'That woman the Duchess. Mother of the sweet little *heiress* to the *throne*. Widow of the sainted Edward. Sainted my arsh! I'm a military man, Mr – whatever you're called. I know the sainted Edward's reputation in the army. Ask Hattersley if he was a white-robed shaint. If you could . . . Hypocrites! Bashtards! Look at how they're treated, and then look at how they behave, what they've *done*. I hate the lot.'

'The Duchess is in a difficult position,' I timidly said.

'Difficult position!' he exploded. 'Bloody wonderful position! Mother to the next queen. Poor old Adelaide would like to find herself in that position! And doesn't the Duchess preen herself! I'd like to wipe that self-satisfied smirk off her face! And I will too! You'll see!'

I had clearly touched a raw nerve, triggered off a naked expression of his ever-present sense of grievance.

'Perhaps you're right,' I said meekly. 'But splendid positions can also be difficult ones.'

104

'Ha! Difficult positions! I'll tell you who are in a difficult position. It's the men and women who are the King's children and are *not* the King's children. It's the men and women who ought to be the highest in the land, but in fact nobody knows quite what they are or how they should be treated. It was difficult for us when my father was a Royal Duke. Now that he's King it's damned impossible! And the one who it's most impossible for is his eldest son, when he thinks what he should be, and sees what he *is*!'

There was a force and a drunken eloquence in what he said. I could not rid myself of the thought that there was something else – something that Lord Melbourne had identified as madness. I tried to calm him.

'I apologise. I should have realised how very difficult things must be for you at the moment.'

'Oh, they're difficult all right. But carefully does it. One step at a time. Feel the way. Does it sound funny, a drunk man talking about taking care? Well it's not. I've taken so much because it's a damned strain, taking care!'

He looked at me through the darkness, his dark eyes glistening. He suddenly seemed to resemble someone I had once known, someone in my own very distant past. He remembered his glass, and downed what smelt like neat brandy, a good inch of it. Then he turned and began staggering back to the castle. I knew better than to follow him. I had got all I was likely to get out of him tonight, I thought. But I was wrong. When he had lurched a few yards he turned back to me.

'I tell you what. Ashk yourshelf why he didn't marry that – that woman till the year 'eighteen. Eh? Eh? Ashk yourshelf.'

I stood, making no reply – knowing of no reply I could make. After a moment he turned and resumed his stumbling progress towards the castle. A drunk man, in a sort of maze, in darkness. It was a miracle he found his way, but he did. As he climbed the steps to the door I heard the sound of glass shattering – he had dropped one of the castle's priceless brandy balloons. No doubt it happened all the time. Then a door opened and shut and I was alone in the darkness.

He was, I could see now, a figure to be pitied. He mingled in Society, which despised him for his illegitimacy. He mingled with the rich, but had himself no fortune. He was the Sovereign's eldest child, and yet a person of no importance. It was a position as different as it could possibly be from the aristocrats with whom he mixed – with a title, an estate, an assumed place in the world that was theirs *by birth*. His birth assured him only trouble and uncertainty, or so it must have seemed to him. It was not to be wondered at if he and the other FitzClarences were determined to make hay while their sun, briefly, shone.

And yet he asked for pity too insistently to get pity. And there was more than that, there was something else behind his self-pity. Raging against the legitimate members of the Royal Family was understandable, chafing at the interest shown in the Heiress Presumptive was natural – and yet there was behind all that something darker and nastier. A mystery, a threat implied, something which I could not fathom, and which probably only drunkenness had brought out.

What in the world could he have meant by asking why the King had not married the Queen until 1818? As far as I knew there had been no lengthy courtship. In fact, I rather thought (my memory is not what it was, and I am in any case not one of those that follow in meticulous detail the doings of the House of Hanover – that way madness lies) that the courtship had been entirely businesslike and epistolary, and that the first time the then Duke of Clarence had clapped eyes on his bride (or, which was perhaps more to the point, vice versa) was when she came over to Britain for the wedding.

Was he implying that his father couldn't marry until his mother Mrs Jordan was dead? She *was* dead by 1818, as far as I remembered. She had been pursued by debt-collectors and had died in obscurity in France some months, I thought, after the Battle of Waterloo. But this was nonsense! No one, to my knowledge, had ever suggested they had been married, and if they had the marriage would have been invalid under the Royal Marriages Act (that foolish measure of the old King that in effect forced his children into adultery – a sin to which they were in any case not averse). He could have married again when he liked. To take a comparative case: having been married to Mrs FitzHerbert hadn't stopped the late unlamented King from marrying his awful Brunswickian legal consort.

What then could he have meant?

I puzzled the question some minutes more, and then made my way carefully along the patterned paths to the eastern front of the castle.

When I let myself into the noble pile it was almost silent. I made my way towards the staircase, eager to hike up it for the last time in a long and tiring day. I was surprised to see, emerging from the doorway and clearly intent on waylaying me, the last figure I would have expected: it was Lord Howe, the Queen's Chamberlain. On his handsome, remote, conceited face was the sort of expression that said that talking to fellows like me was something that as a rule he would prefer to leave to his servants.

'Mr . . . er . . . Mozart?'

I bowed.

'Lord Howe?'

He had to repress a grimace, as if somehow I had made free with his name, which should have remained sacred and unvoiced, as Jehovah is among the Jewish.

'If I may have a moment, Mr . . . Mozart. I gather from Her Majesty that you are engaged on a matter of some delicacy for the King.' I remained silent. 'I would not of course want to trespass on your discretion, naturally not, but I do want to assure you of my complete co-operation in every way.'

I bowed again.

'I am much obliged to Your Lordship.'

'The Duke of Cumberland, as you know, is of my party, and a man of excellent and steadfast Conservative principles.' I made no response to this. His party was not mine, and was an irrelevance. 'However, I have a higher loyalty than party loyalty, and that is to the Royal House.'

'I think we all have that loyalty, Lord Howe.'

I can bootlick with the highest in the land. I've done it all my life. However, he bowed in a way that seemed to doubt the quality of my loyalty, or its value.

'The Duke's behaviour this afternoon was contemptible and ridiculous . . . I noticed you go out on to the terrace. I believe George FitzClarence was out there as well.'

'He was.' I took a sudden decision, not to trust him, but to use him. 'May I ask, Lord Howe, if there is any history of . . . of mental instability in that case?'

He pursed his lips.

'Rashness, choler, great unwisdom. He ruined his military career by a combination of such qualities – and it was, by all accounts, a promising career. But madness, no. On the other hand the accession of his father—'

'Understood, My Lord. There is no need to put it into words.' I paused, to choose my words with care. This was a delicate subject. 'His mother, I seem to remember, died soon after the Continental Wars ended.'

'In eighteen-sixteen.' He mentioned her as if she were a bad taste in his mouth.

'I never remember any talk of there having been a marriage ceremony between his mother and his father.'

He became very frosty.

'There was none. This is naturally not a matter I could take up with the King—'

'Naturally not.'

'—but I think I can say without fear of contradiction that there was not. In any case such a ceremony would have been invalid.'

'Of course it would. But to a mind diseased . . . It is all very puzzling. The King and Mrs Jordan had in fact separated some time before, I seem to remember.'

'Yes, in eighteen-eleven.'

'Yet the King did not marry the present Queen until eighteen-eighteen?'

'There were . . . attempts. Best not spoken of.'

'Of course, of course . . . There is one other matter you may be able to help me with, My Lord.'

He inclined his head infinitesimally.

'The late Duke of Kent. What was his connection with a man called Hattersley?'

He nodded, perfectly in command of the matter.

'He was an insubordinate and unruly soldier in the regiment the Duke commanded in Gibraltar. He died after punishment.'

'Ah,' I said.

Oh really? I thought.

TWELVE

Picnic

I slept the sleep of the just, whether or not I deserved it. Though I suppose exhaustion in the service of the King (or, rather more particularly, a tiny, threatened, though not entirely defenceless Princess) would traditionally be considered a noble cause. It was difficult though to see myself in the role of knight errant so popular with writers of the present medieval school. I awoke shortly before nine greatly refreshed, took some time over my *toilette* – though probably nowhere near as much time as the fine ladies of the party – and then sallied out in search of people, news, further enlightenment.

I first went in quest of the room where poor old Popper had died. This was not easy, but as with a maze that one thinks one will never find one's way out of but eventually does, I did at last come upon the room. There was no sign of life there, nor any of death: it was empty, the bed unmade. Only a faint smell of disinfectant told me that someone had been at work scrubbing away the stench of vomit and death. A very under-footman, a mere apprentice at the castle's lack-of-charm school, told me that Mr Nussey was in attendance on one of the housemaids. I demurred at entering the servants' quarters, fearing either to lose my way again in a still worse warren of corridors, or else to encounter things that would shock the sensibilities even of a man of the theatre (for the King had inherited his servants from his predecessor, and it is notorious that the moral tone below stairs is taken from the moral tone above them). I therefore charged the footman with a message to the good apothecary saying that I would wait for him on the terrace. The man did my bidding with the merest suspicion of a sniff. He would learn.

I turned and made my way back through the corridors, which were beginning to show signs of life. As I started down the wider corridors close to the stairs I saw hurrying towards me the Princess's maid.

'Oh, Mrs Hattersley—'

'Mr Mozart, I canna tarry. There's talk of a picnic.'

'Of a *what?*'

'The King's sent a message to the Princess. He's planning a picnic for the children and all the folks else, in the Great Park. Though what the Duchess will say when she gets wind of it, the Guid Lord kens.'

I let her bustle on. She would keep. She could surely be no more than a minor piece in the puzzle. Her news, however, was upsetting, and I descended the staircase in a worried state of mind. The project of the King was typical of him, in his desire to give pleasure to children – particularly to children like the Princess, for whom pleasure was a scarce commodity. It was also typical of him that, where his family was concerned, common sense tended to fly out the window.

On duty at the foot of the stairs was the unfrocked Bishop, standing immobile, seeming impervious to any signs of humanity in the rooms around him, the only evidence of life in him being the occasional wobble of his formidable double chin. He looked like a statue Mr Gillray might have carved, if he had had talent in that art. I screwed my courage to the sticking place and approached his majesty.

'The Great Park is now open to the public, is it not?'

Yes, sir,' he said, from a great height. 'The present . . . King reversed the decision of the late King, and the terraces and the park are now open to the . . . *pub*lic.'

Along with the other vermin of the insect and animal kingdom, his manner implied.

'Every day of the week?'

'Every day except Friday, sir. Today is Friday.'

I refrained with difficulty from bowing, and walked through the door and down the steps to the terrace and garden. I reflected on the odd fate that made a castle footman (however majestic) one of the few who were privy not just to the death that had taken place last night, but to our suspicions of what lay behind it. The King, myself, Mr Nussey – and the unfrocked Bishop. And did that mean the whole regiment of castle servants? And if so did that mean the visiting servants as well? If so it could only be a matter of time before the grand guests at Windsor knew of our suspicions as well.

I paced the terrace and looked out on to the Great Park. It looked from that point as if the picnic party would be easy to guard. In fact there was already a member of the Household Cavalry by one of the gateways in the railings, and I could see in the distance (or thought I could, because my eyesight is by no means what it was) a party of gardeners and groundsmen inspecting coppices and ha-has for intruders left over from the day before. All to the good: the King was concerned about his niece's safety. Or just possibly he was anxious to allay the perfectly justifiable fears of the Duchess of Kent. Either way my own anxieties for the safety of the Princess would now restrict themselves to the present denizens of the castle – inhabitants, guests, domestic staff.

'Mr Mozart?'

I was standing at the parapet where I had stood with George FitzClarence the night before. Mr Nussey came busily up, the much-in-demand family doctor to the life, but mixing ingratiation with his self-importance to a degree he would only do when attending at a royal palace. I think I was in his good books for having introduced him to the King, but I didn't expect it to last. He was not the sort of professional man likely to give a proper respect to artistic genius.

'Ah, Mr Nussey,' I said, somewhat commandingly for me. 'I wanted to be *au courant* with what has gone on. I note that the body has been moved.'

'It has indeed,' he said, with immense self-satisfaction. '*Re*moved, in fact. On the orders of the King.' His voice was hushed, though we were alone on the terrace. 'Four members of the castle staff removed it in the early hours, Mr Mozart. Such a death at the castle would never have done at all. The body has been transported to London, to Mr Popper's abode.'

'I see.'

'Was Mr Popper married?'

'No, he was not married.'

'Good, good.' He rubbed his hands. 'Then there will only be his servants to cope with.'

I did not enlighten him on Mr Popper's domestic arrangements, which included a shrew of a mistress who had once played small roles at the Queen's Theatre, a woman who made Mr Popper's home so hot that not a member of the present Queen's company would go near it. I did not doubt she would make trouble, but equally I did not doubt she could be bought off.

'So all trace of Mr Popper has disappeared from the castle?'

'It has, it has. A most satisfactory outcome.'

'Except for Mr Popper. And for the fact that it still remains to find out how he died.'

'Oh, I have little doubt about that, Mr Mozart. Digitalis, or one of its derivatives.'

'But the question remains how he came to ingest – I believe that is the word you use – it, does it not?'

'Oh, I could have no opinion as to that,' he said, apparently unconcerned. 'That is for you to find out, Mr Mozart.'

He bowed a thankful farewell, leaving me with the problem very much as it had been before our conversation. I stood meditating for a few minutes, watching the preparations gathering momentum in the Great Park (it is a very special kind of picnic that needs a posse of groundsmen and cavalry to prepare for it), then turned and made my way back indoors.

Inside the castle preparations for the picnic seemed to have taken over the whole grandiose pile. Footmen and butlers, maids and housekeepers were scurrying hither and thither, like the poet Milton's thousands who 'post o'er land and ocean without rest'. The King was bustling about too, giving the impression that he had to supervise everything himself, and was even capable of making the sandwiches if necessary, as very possibly he was. Lady Erroll was watching him with a smile on her face, as if this was something she was very used to from her childhood. The Duchess of Kent was there, fuming with suppressed irritation and doubt, but the King mostly coped with her objections by ignoring them, though he did at one point say in passing, 'Much better out in the open, you know. No walls or dark corners. She can be watched all the time.'

112

There were quite obvious ways of countering this argument, but he did not give her the opportunity, merely bumbling on and shouting commands and encouragements to all and sundry, footmen, staff and castle guests. He could have been on the quarterdeck of some rather jolly ship. I noticed that one or two of the footmen, though not all by any means, were losing a layer or two of starchiness and entering into the spirit of the thing. It wasn't what they were used to under the previous King, but it was quite enjoyable, and when all was said and done the Princess Sophia was right: kingliness is what the King does.

'*Isn't* the King enjoying himself?' came a wistful voice at my side, and I turned and saw the Princess Victoria.

'He loves giving pleasure,' I agreed, 'which is a nice change. He especially likes giving pleasure to children.'

'I wish there were more people like that,' she said meaningfully. 'All I hear about is *duty* . . . It won't be my duty to be with George Cambridge all the time at the picnic, will it? That would make it a very dull treat.'

'I'm sure not,' I said, though I had no idea what the Duchess had in mind for her daughter. 'It's a pity we have no actresses to occupy his attention,' the Princess giggled, 'but I'm sure you can be with whomever you like.

'The Countess of Erroll is *lovely,*' said the Princess, looking in her direction, the wistful note in her voice again. 'Wouldn't it be wonderful if I was lovely like that? A new young queen who was also beautiful. It would drive people mad with loyalty to the throne. But I suppose I shall just have to be nice, or virtuous, or good, or something.'

'Don't let the King hear you talking about being Queen, or he'll think you're numbering his days.'

She threw up her chin.

'Don't treat me as entirely foolish and thoughtless, Mr Mozart. *Other people* do that, but you know better. I do know how to behave.' The obstinate expression lasted long enough to make an effect. Then she smiled. 'There, that's over. I can be terribly grumpy if I try. It's my only weapon against Mama.'

By about eleven o'clock the bustle had sorted itself out into something like order, and it was time for us all to sally forth. The Duchess of Kent was clearly very reluctant, but there was

113

still some remnant of awe for the new King, and she had to make the best of a bad job. I saw her murmur instructions to Baroness Lehzen, and as we all left the castle, traversed the terrace and went down into the park I saw that Lehzen had the Princess by the hand and was keeping it determinedly in hers. The Princess obviously found this most demeaning, and looked very cross, or grumpy as she would call it. I had the impression, though, that she was biding her time.

A house party at Windsor Castle picnicking in the Great Park was a little like a family in a less grand residence picnicking in their back yard. However, the park was large enough for there to be plenty of spots for all tastes and pursuits – sunny spots and shady spots, open places and secret places. True to his remarks to the Duchess the King chose open lawn to set out the cloths and hampers. In any case his weather-beaten complexion showed that he liked the sun (it could not still be weather-beaten from his sea-going days), but this liking was not shared by the more genteel members of his court: ladies shielded their milky complexions under large hats and veils, and one could even see fine gentlemen making for the shade of trees. A tanned skin would never do: it might suggest that one worked in the open air!

The Princess was not after all to be burdened with the company of George Cambridge. He attached himself to the Queen, being a great favourite of hers, and they got round them a little knot of Erroll grandchildren. The King devoted himself to the very small FitzClarences, watched delightedly by the Princess Victoria.

'What you have to watch for on picnics,' he was telling them, 'are the creepy-crawlies.'

'What's keepy kawlies, Grandad King?' asked a fine-looking little boy.

'Creepy-crawlies are things that live in the earth, little tiny creatures, and they love sandwiches and buns and all good things like that, and when we open the hampers and sit down to eat they come creepy-crawling out of the earth – ' he was on his knees, suiting the action to the words – 'and they sniff jam sandwiches and the icing on currant buns and they come creepy-crawling over to have their share.'

114

And he snatched an imaginary currant bun from the hands of the little FitzClarence boy. The Princess Victoria laughed heartily, and the little FitzClarences crowed with delight. I saw the King looking, rather pathetically, to his son for approval, but George FitzClarence was brooding some feet away, and showed no sign of noticing what was going on around him. I have seldom known anyone who spent so much time *within himself.*

I came up behind the Baroness Lehzen, standing some feet away, her eyes watching everything that was going on in the little group through wire spectacles perched on a nose so sharp it could serve as a chisel.

'The Princess is enjoying herself, Baroness,' I said.

'Yes,' she said shortly. 'It is good from time to time.'

'It is good for her to have children to play with, too, instead of adults.'

'It is good,' she agreed. 'It is not easy.'

'Oh?'

'There is not many childrens who are on an equality with her.'

'Don't you think children make their own equality?'

She shook her head solemnly.

'That is not good. She must think of her future, of her duty, of her great position.'

I refrained from demurring, but the idea of a child sitting around thinking of her duty, her future and her great position the whole time was a daunting one.

'At any rate she can enjoy herself today. Watched over by us.'

She bridled visibly.

'*I* shall vatch her. It is not necessary you concern yourself, Mr Mozart.'

'Two watchdogs are better than one,' I said equably, ignoring her obvious jealousy.

As it happened my own attention was diverted at that moment. I saw coming towards us from the gate in the railings just beyond the Long Walk – the gate that led to the town of Windsor – the Princess Sophia and the man I now knew to be her son: she was talking unconstrainedly. He appeared to listen, but his eyes went everywhere, whether to

115

take in the details of the royal picnic or looking for someone or something specific I could not tell.

This was a blow. I looked towards the King but he, by popular demand, was doing a repeat performance as a creepy-crawly, to immense applause. In any case I don't suppose he would have welcomed any looks of reproach I might direct at him. Kings come to like applause and approbation, and they are liable to withdraw favour from those who don't give it to them. I was too little used to royal patronage, too sensible of the tangible benefits flowing from it, to risk its being withdrawn.

'I had assumed the picnic was to be restricted to guests at the castle,' I murmured to Baroness Lehzen. 'But that gentleman is certainly not one of them.'

She looked in the direction I pointed, clearly not knowing who or what he was, or possibly (which was very worrying) not being able to see who it was.

'I shall be on vatch for *every*one,' she pronounced complacently. 'It is necessary.'

I, having no more than the usual number of eyes, found that I had to make a choice as to who I watched. My task was made easier, however, by the fact that the King gestured to the flunkeys who were in attendance (they did not include the Bishop – bishops don't go on picnics), and the hampers were opened, plates and glasses were placed around the shining white table-cloths, and the guzzling part of the picnic began in earnest.

The children were best at the guzzling, of course. There were indeed jam sandwiches and sticky currant buns, as well as every kind of cake, biscuit and sweet pastry imaginable: gingerbread, treacle sponge, seed cake, fruit cake and unlimited sweetmeats. It was no doubt very bad for them, which was why they enjoyed it so much. The adults were less wholehearted in entering into the spirit of the party. The patés and the cold tongue and the game pie were all delicious – I was eating, in fact, at Windsor as I had never eaten in my life before – but they were not the sort of adults who were used to picnics or could be easy at them. The gaiety was forced and spasmodic, and we spent much time commenting on the uproarious joy of the children, whose fun was led by the King and Queen, who seemed more

116

able than anyone to forget their Great Position. I was fortunate in sitting next to Princess Sophia rather than, say, Lord Howe, who stuck out like a spider at a flies' feast.

'*Don't* William and Adelaide do this sort of thing well?' the Princess commented to me in low tones. 'If only their little girl had lived.'

I dared to sound out her opinion of her fellow residents at Kensington.

'Yes, they would certainly be more sympathetic parents than ... some others,' I said. She smiled understandingly.

'The poor Duchess tries, but much too hard, and she never will take advice to let up, give Victoria more freedom, more company she can be a little girl with.' She paused, then added, 'Though she probably thinks it's absurd that I should be offering advice about bringing up children.' My eyes involuntarily went to the figure of Tom Garth at the next cover. 'Ah, you know?'

'The King did ... mention the relationship.'

'I expect everyone knows.'

'Baroness Lehzen didn't seem to know who he was.'

'Lehzen is single-minded and rather stupid. Her only interest is Princess Victoria. One day she will become a great nuisance ... William means well, of course, and thinks he is giving me a great treat, but really you know we have nothing to say to each other. Nothing in the world. I found that yesterday, when he came – reluctantly – on to the terrace with me. I chattered on, he tried to respond, but we had nothing in common. Not even a shared past, which is what most parents and children have. When we were watching your little piece he had much more to say to George FitzClarence, and I would have felt hurt, but then I thought: but it's perfectly natural – they *do* have plenty in common.'

At that moment I caught a glance – a glance of complicity – from Tom Garth on one side of the table-cloth next to ours to George FitzClarence on the other. A line of Shakespeare sprang to my mind – another line such as probably did not get into the Princess Victoria's edition of the Bard:

'Now, gods, stand up for bastards!'

THIRTEEN
Lessons in Love

There is this to be said for royal picnics, even when the partici-
pants are a stiff-necked lot: they have not been frequent enough
to develop an etiquette of their own, so that by and large one
can do pretty much what one wants. The natural progression
of eating and then sleeping, which is difficult or impossible at
a formal banquet, can come about quite naturally at a picnic.

The wine had been light, but of a superb quality, and the
King knocked it back enthusiastically.

'Damned good wine!' he would say, looking around him for
approval. 'Better than I've ever been able to afford. There's this
to be said for m'brother: he had taste. Damned expensive taste,
but good.'

Accordingly, when the last traces of the wonderful comestibles
were being cleared away by the army of silent footmen, and even
as the Queen was fussing around him and talking about possible
chills and the dampness getting on his chest, the King lay back
on the grass and in a couple of seconds was snoring contentedly.
A great many of the adult members of the party followed suit.

I would have liked to be one of those, but I felt too keenly my
obligation to keep guard over the Princess Victoria. Baroness
Lehzen too, though it was clear that sun and wine had produced
a desperate desire to nod off, battled to stay awake and keep
watch. The Duchess battled a similar inclination, watching the
children's games and frolics, her mouth set in a straight, hard
line as she realised she was powerless to prevent her daughter
playing with the little Errolls and FitzClarences – was far from
sure, probably, which they were.

I was more interested in their parents, or rather one of them.

118

Lady Erroll was sleeping beautifully on a grassy bank, while her husband was playing a quarrelsome game of poker with two other gentlemen and making the air fragrant with his excellent cigar. But George FitzClarence was standing under a tree a little way into what remained of the forest – standing on the other side of the trunk, away from the company, so that I only knew it was he because the shoulders of his distinctive and dashing blue coat were visible. I was convinced there was also someone else there, but of him or her I could get no glimpse. I kept my eyes on the tree behind which he was standing, only occasionally switching to Princess Victoria, who had left the tumbling group of small children and was exchanging dutiful words with George Cambridge. I was convinced I could hear a faint trickle of conversation from the forest, then a distant laugh which was not George FitzClarence's desperate, almost maniacal laugh. A blue-clad arm was suddenly visible, putting something into the pocket of the coat. Then a shape disappeared further into the depths of the forest, and FitzClarence came out from the shadow of the trees, standing for a moment, almost posing, on the edge of the grass. Pictures could have been painted of him by Sir Thomas Lawrence or Sir David Wilkie: *The Hope of the Nation*, or *The King's Heir*. If only . . .

His shoulder relaxed, his head was let off duty, and he turned away from the company, took from his pocket a folded sheet of paper and began to study it intently. I found I desperately wanted to find out what it was.

A thought occurred to me: the Princess, so tiny and quiet, might well be able to discover what I almost certainly could not manage. I took out a tiny notebook I keep with me to note down musical ideas when they occur to me (still they occur to me, after nearly seventy years' composing!) and wrote:

> M.D. It would interest me extremely to find out what is in the paper which George FitzClarence has been reading so intently.
>
> Mr. M.

M.D. was my improvised code for 'my dear'. I thought the Princess would puzzle it out, and enjoy doing it. It did occur

119

to me that I might be putting her in a position of danger, but I dismissed the idea: I would watch her every movement. She was by now back with the rest of the children, playing a vigorous game of Ring o' Roses with a clutch of the King's grandchildren. I tore the page from my notebook and concealed it in my hand.

'De Princess will get tired and overheated, ma'am,' I heard Lehzen call to the Duchess of Kent. I thought that one thing the little girl needed was to get tired and overheated now and then, but I immediately stood up.

'I will fetch her.'

Black look from the Baroness Lehzen.

By the time I came up to the noisy knot of children they were approaching another climax of the Ring, and they all fell down with a tremendous soprano roar. The Princess was flushed and laughing. I bent my head towards her.

'Your governess thinks that you may be getting tired and overheated, Your Royal Highness.'

She pushed out her lower lip still further.

'Oh, bother Lehzen!' she began, but I gave her a slow and significant wink and held out my hand. She put her hand into mine, and I heard a little chuckle as she felt the folded paper in the palm. She gave no more trouble about joining the grown-ups, merely saying conversationally, 'I wouldn't have thought it possible but I had a *most* interesting conversation with George Cambridge about being in love. It seems a most de*light*ful state of mind, from his account. Have you been often in love, Mr Mozart?'

I was saved from the need to reply: the last roar of the children as they all fell down had arounsed the King from his noisy slumbers.

'What? What?' he said, sitting up and looking around him. 'You've been asleep, m'dear,' he said to his Queen, who was sitting quietly beside him, probably wondering how to prevent the damp going to his chest. Then the King gave a loud laugh. 'May have nodded off m'self.' He stood up and strode over to the children. 'Cricket, eh? Time for cricket, don't you think? We always had cricket at Bushey.'

I don't know what you think about cricket. To me it is a

peculiarly English (or Englishly peculiar) game. I don't see any other nation or race taking it up (I gather it is never played in the former colonies of America, where the climate is much more suitable for it). However, I suppose it is preferable as a sport to prize-fighting, around which the patronage of the late Lord Byron has put a false romantic aura, but which to my mind is a reversion to barbarism.

As a matter of fact the game of cricket, as improvised by the King (though he had had the foresight to order bats and balls to be brought, including very small bats and soft balls) bore little relationship to the tedious rituals of the village green – this game being very noisy and harmless, as well as a good deal faster. Perhaps it was my memory of those previous games, witnessed in small towns where I had inadvertently got myself stranded after a concert or a recital, but whatever the reason something for a short time sent me off to sleep. I was stretched forward on my stomach like some schoolboy from Eton, the educational establishment nearby, and I remember noticing that the Princess was not far away and that, her mother's and her governess's eyes being on the cricket game, she had opened and was reading my note. I met her eye, smiled at her, then my head must have fallen down on to my outstretched arms and I dozed.

I awoke suddenly, perhaps prodded by a passing foot or aroused by a worrying dream. The Princess was nowhere to be seen. I sat up sharply and turned away from the cricket game, slowly but urgently surveying the expanse of the park. At last I saw her: she was between us and the castle, but she was approaching from behind the figure of George FitzClarence, solitary as he so often was (it almost seemed symbolic of his state), and standing, paper in hand, alternately looking at it, then letting his hand drop and meditating on what he had been reading, or re-reading rather. My first impulse was to jump up and rush over to protect the Princess. At once I told myself that this was absurd: it was I who had sent her on that mission in the first place. My reason was unsettled by my sleep, and by the feeling that I had fallen down on my duty, like a sleeping sentry. Not that I was the only one: Lehzen was fast asleep, and looking round I soon established that neither the

Duchess of Kent nor Sir John Conroy was there to keep an eye on the Princess.

But now I was alert again and could watch. The Princess, so small and delicate, approached him from behind, concealing her stealth with an insouciant manner. She had, I knew from her lessons with me, good eyesight. She stood there, mute, trying to scan the paper, helped by his tallness and her own diminutive size, for when he was not looking at it his hand with the paper in it was not far from her eyes. Something in the set of her shoulders told me that she was frustrated, probably by the fact that the side of the paper presented to her was blank. She stood thoughtful for a moment, and then started round into the man's view.

I could, of course, hear nothing, only watch their movements. When he became conscious of her he started and looked down. She spoke to him and he replied: she spoke again and he looked away, then seemed to say something. As soon as he took his eyes off her the Princess's eyes dropped to the paper in his hand. She went on talking I think, but quite suddenly he looked down, snatched the paper away from her eyes and stuffed it into his pocket. They talked on for a few moments more, then I heard a burst of laughter from George FitzClarence, and he began striding away from her in the direction of the cricket match.

'Sometimes I worry about George,' said a voice at my side and, turning, I saw that it was the Countess of Erroll, now beautifully awake and contemplating the scene I had just witnessed. I was about to ask her what she meant when I saw that the Princess, who had watched her departing cousin, perhaps telling herself how *won*derfully handsome he was, had turned away from us and had begun walking in the direction of the outskirts of the forest.

I stood up as fast as my old limbs would allow me to, gave a hasty bow to the Countess, and began in the same direction. Even with George FitzClarence well out of the way I was not happy at the thought of the Princess wandering in the shadow of the forest away from all observing eyes. But into the forest she went, and by the time I had reached the path by which she had entered there was not a glimpse to be had of her tiny figure or her pretty white dress. I started in, very uncertain of

122

my course of action. Should I shout, rush to get people to look for her? Would it not seem absurd? A child in a wood is not necessarily in danger. I walked on, trying to cool my agitation. Some way in the paths forked. Which one to take? I am *very* inexperienced in forests – indeed, I never remember being in one before, in spite of the fact that the final scene of my last, unperformed opera takes place in this very forest. I am a townsman, and I stopped, irresolute.

I thought I heard a crackle of twigs to my right. I began that way, but very tentatively, for I knew, even as a townsman, that one can easily be misled by the apparent direction of noises. Almost at once I was rewarded by a flash of white in the distance, then by the sight of the little figure walking fast and determinedly in my direction. I stopped, took a deep breath, and made a decision not to make a 'fuss', something she would hate. I was troubled to see when she came closer that her charming little pig face was very red, and her eyes were filled with tears – not of sadness, I thought, but of something else I could not identify. Was it anger? Something like shame? She looked as if she wanted nothing more than to find a place where she could hide and have a long, wonderfully relieving cry. But that would not have been a good idea. I held out my hand to her. She looked up at me as if she was seeing me for the first time. Then, without smiling, she took my hand and together we walked in silence along the pathways and out of the forest.

'It's absolutely disgusting!' she burst out when we were safely out in the open, her words contrasting with her girlish, bell-like tones.

'Oh?' I said neutrally.

'There will be no need for you to make any more enquiries, Mr Mozart. I have *seen* them!'

'I see.' I took some moments to digest this information. It was a very delicate matter, because it could be thought improper to ask her what she had seen them doing. However, it seemed unlikely, in the context of a well-attended royal picnic, that they were doing very much.

'This was your Mama and Sir John?' I asked at last.

'Of course.'

'And they were?—'

'Kissing. Under a tree. So you see I *know*.'

Her face was red, her eyes angry, as if she felt both humiliated and confused by what she had seen.

'You say you *know*, my dear. But what do you know?'

'That they are lovers.'

I was in a quandary again. There seemed to be no way of enlightening her about the significance of that phrase without enlightening her on several biological matters of which she was obviously ignorant – and it was hardly my place to do that. After some deliberation I stopped, turned her round to look at me, and said, 'What you know, my dear, is that they feel affection for each other.'

'Yes – they're lovers. It's disgusting.'

'But when you talked to your cousin Prince George you thought love a delightful state.'

She frowned, more confused than ever.

'But that's quite different. Of course it seemed a delightful state, because we were talking about young people. But at their age! And in Mama's position!'

'I'm afraid love pays little regard to age or position.'

'But Mama should certainly pay regard to it. She has already had two husbands. Is that not enough?'

'Your Mama is a healthy and handsome woman.'

'And Sir John is a healthy and handsome man. That does not make it *right*.'

We had come up to where the Baroness Lehzen was sleeping soundly on the grass. I was uncertain what to do, but the Princess, with the familiarity of long experience, shook her awake. She opened her eyes and struggled to a sitting position.

'I am taking the Princess back to the castle,' I explained. 'She is a little tired.'

'But how can she have got tired? I have been vatching her all de time.'

The Princess let out a silvery laugh, kissed her governess (something I would not have cared to do), and we began our long walk back to the castle watched by a very bad-tempered Lehzen. The Princess's laugh may have betokened a return to her customary mood, but she was by no means ready to leave the subject of her mother. We had not gone many steps before that little chin tilted upwards again.

'Mama should forfeit the right to be my guardian!'

I regretted having to pour cold water on so much of what she said, but I had no alternative.

'That would be a matter for Parliament, and I'm sure they would be very reluctant to separate a mother and daughter.'

'But mothers do lose the right to their children if they are guilty of adulthood.'

I had noticed before that the Princess tended to confuse adulthood and adultery. I suppose with her family the confusion was natural.

'Adultery is not what you saw, my dear. Adultery is much more serious. Besides, who would become your guardian?'

'The King and Queen, of course!'

That was a plausible, natural and extremely dangerous notion.

'The King and Queen have many new duties, as well as many older ones in connection with the King's children.' (Who, I was beginning to agree with the Duchess, should be kept well out of the Princess's way.)

'George Cambridge stays with them almost all the time,' she said, with an obsessive pursuit of a fixed idea that I was beginning to recognise as part of her character. 'He says the Queen is very kind and the King is very jolly.'

'I'm sure they are, my dear. They both love children. But a natural bond is a natural bond, and mother and daughter should not be separated unless there is a *very* good reason.'

'There *is* good reason.' She saw from my face that I did not agree with her, and she was conscious that she was entering on to ground of which she felt very uncertain. She modified her attitude. 'Well, if I can't go and live with the King and Queen, I shall at least get my own way with Mama.'

'Oh?'

'I shall tell her what I saw and she will *have* to let me do as I want.'

I raised my eyebrows and shook my head, feeling the most awful wet blanket.

'Well, Your Royal Highness, I will not deny that you have a very powerful weapon.'

'Thank you, Mr Mozart. I know I do.'

'But a good commander does not use his cannon in a minor skirmish. He saves it for the big battle. Ask the Duke of Wellington if you don't believe me – but don't, for heaven's sake, tell him *why* you are asking.'

She giggled – a good sign – and thought about this as we toiled up on to the terraces of the castle.

'You mean that I should not tell her what I saw until there is a very important matter in which I need to get my own way?'

'That is exactly what I mean,' I replied, hoping fervently that she would hoard the knowledge so well that the important matter would not arise until after she had come of age. 'But we have been talking about this so much that you have not told me about George FitzClarence and your talk with him.'

It was not to be. We were nearing the east front, and by that mysterious communication between servants (I knew not whether this was innate and habitual to the Windsor staff or induced by special instructions of the King) word of our impending arrival had been transmitted to Mrs Hattersley, who now issued forth to take charge of the Princess as if she were at best long-lost or at worst had been kidnapped.

'Don't fuss, Elspeth,' said the Princess, but the fuss at least served to disguise from her loyal but officious servant her troubled state of mind.

Discontentedly I roamed the castle, where lounged members of the party who had shirked the picnic – playing billiards in obscure parts of the old pile, or gossiping in gilded corners. I was surprised when I strayed into the Waterloo Chamber to be buttonholed by the Duke of Wellington, who had never before favoured me with a word in his life (most appropriate setting for him, as he was probably surveying the portraits of old friends and enemies whom he very likely despised equally and impartially). He is a man who knows no more of music than the King – in his case his knowledge is probably limited to marches as the King's is to hornpipes and shanties. But talk to me, in his stiff way, he did, and we were soon joined by Lord Melbourne, who I suspect had left the picnic as soon as he saw the Princess coming away.

'The Princess enjoyed herself?' he enquired solicitously, and soon we were deep in the topic that was making me such a popular visitor to the castle.

'I was saying to Mr Mozart yesterday,' said Lord Melbourne, addressing the Duke, 'that it will be such *fun* when she is Queen. And I shan't live to see it!'

'Still less I,' said the Duke. 'Unless the King's asthma takes him off early.'

'I think a court presided over by the Duchess of Kent would not be great fun,' I ventured. The Duke and Lord Melbourne looked at one another.

'A Regency for the Duchess is not to be taken for granted,' said the Duke. 'Whatever the complexion of the government.'

'No, indeed,' agreed Lord Melbourne. 'There's Sussex and there's Cambridge.'

'The Duke of Cambridge is the only one of the Dukes who has never been a millstone round the public neck,' said the Duke. Then, remembering he was talking to me, he added, quite mendaciously, 'Except the King, of course. Cambridge has brains and he has feelings that do him credit.'

'Do you know the Princess's sentiments concerning a Regency?' Lord Melbourne asked me.

'The Princess had *very* much rather the question never arises,' I said, as forcibly as I could. 'She feels the awkwardness of it acutely, particularly if things are done in her name of which she does not approve.'

'Sensible as well as great fun,' said Lord Melbourne. 'Long may she live and reign.'

'And save us from the Duke of Cumberland,' said the Duke feelingly.

'Amen to that,' agreed Lord Melbourne. 'We on our side have no reason to love him.'

'Nor we on ours,' said the Duke, with that unanimity of feeling that Cumberland always evokes. 'He was insufferable about Catholic Emancipation. And he made the last months of the late King's life a complete misery.'

'I don't suppose there was ever much prospect of their being very happy.'

'That doesn't excuse him badgering a dying man.'

'True. If the Duke were heir to the throne both parties would really have to come together to save the nation from him.'

So there I was mixing with the Highest in the Land and discussing the character of the Heiress Presumptive and the next heir after her! Strange transformation in my fortunes! We went on for some time, but soon the picnicking party drifted back, and it was time to dress for dinner. I was pleased but not altogether surprised to find on the little table in my bedroom, tucked under my bowl and my jug of lukewarm water, a note. It was addressed in a spluttering pen on the envelope M.D.O.F. I took this to mean My Dear Old Friend, and was flattered and unworried by the thought that, in the circumstances, Old could only signify 'aged'. I opened it and read.

'The schocking seen that I witnessed in the forest today put out of my head the matter you wanted me to find out about. The paper in Goerge Fitsclarence's hand was some sort of copie from a rejister, as of birth or a death perhaps. But I could not see it close, and to see it at all I had to go round and talk to him. I askt him if he was enjoying the picnic, and he said that his children were enjoying it very much and picnics were for children. Saying which he *looked* at me and his expresion was not nice, as if he hated me (as pehaps he may, I being lejitimate and he NOT!) Then he looked away quickly so I could not see his face, and that was when I saw the paper. I said he seemed to have a lot to consern him, and he said he did. Then he saw me pearing at the paper and snatched it away. I said was it matters of state that conserned him (tho I knew it could not be, he having no posishion) and he looked at me and said you might say that, and then he thought and said yes, you could say this will be very much a matter of state.

Then he burst out into his horrible laugh which I do not like at all, and walked away (rather *rudely*).

I hope I have done well, M.D.O.F.

Yours greatfully

128

She did not sign it. I suppose she hoped that, if it were found, it could be thought to be from any of the great ladies at the castle. But on the whole I thought she had done very well indeed.

FOURTEEN

Shadows of the Past

I went down to dinner that night, the last dinner of the duchess's stay at the castle, with new confidence. I was conscious as always that I was not so well dressed (though natty) as the rest, not so well groomed, not so exquisitely perfumed. But I also knew that the King's patronage of me and reliance on me – and I suspected there was a great deal of conjecture as to its cause and its nature – had made me a figure to be noted, even courted. I was no longer a mere hanger-on to the theatrical performers.

I was placed at table between Lord Erroll and Lord Melbourne, both figures of consequence, you will note. Talk was freer that evening, perhaps loosened by the picnic, or by the fact that people were imperceptibly getting to know each other better, and even the courtiers were shaking down into the more free-and-easy manners of the new reign. The fact that talk was more general enabled me to have a short but *sotto voce* conversation of a 'business' nature with Lord Melbourne.

'My Lord, do you remember the time when the present King began his . . . association with the mother of his children?'

He looked at me with the look of a shrewd politician – that is the look that says every question has a motive behind it.

'Hardly. I remember talk. But I was a mere boy at the time. You yourself will remember better, Mr Mozart.'

There is a streak of vanity in my Lord Melbourne that made him emphasise his greater youth, though I think I can say without fear of contradiction that few people observing us would suspect a difference of twenty or so years between us. Lord Melbourne is a handsome but not *young* fifty-or-so-year-old.

130

Perhaps the fact that I had the happiest of marriages to my dear Connie, while Lord Melbourne was yoked to a demented maenad, the paramour of Lord Byron, accounts for our appearances as men very much of the same age.

'But you, My Lord, mingled in aristocratic circles, where his doings were likely to be the subject of comment.'

'But you mixed in theatrical circles, Mr Mozart.'

'In those circles there was talk, of course. But such things, in the theatre, are very much a matter of course.'

'As they are in aristocratic circles as well.'

I dipped my head, smiling broadly.

'I take your point, My Lord. If there was no great fuss in theatrical circles it may be because Mrs Jordan was the discreetest of women. Whereas His Majesty . . .'

'Ah, quite.'

'I was wondering if, at the time, there was any talk of a form of marriage having been contracted between them.'

He raised his eyebrows and let out a little 'phew' of astonishment. I could see that he was both remembering and examining the motive behind the question.

'None that I can remember,' he said, frowning. 'There was talk at home, there was talk at Eton, where the doings of the King's sons were naturally the subject of gossip – and some envy. But I never remember talk of any *marriage*. Of course any such marriage would have been illegal.'

'Naturally,' I agreed readily. 'Under the Royal Marriages Act the pair would have had to have the permission of the King, which they certainly would not have got. But I wondered whether the Duke – the King, as is – perhaps from some feelings of chivalry, might have gone through some such ceremony.'

Lord Melbourne lowered his voice still further.

'The King hasn't the feelings of a gentleman. He knows what they are, but he hasn't got them. I would doubt it very much.'

'As a protest, then, at the King's tyranny over his own family, and the restrictions of the Royal Marriages Act?'

'That is just possible,' conceded Lord Melbourne. 'Some such feelings, mixed with others, were probably behind the marriage ceremonies gone through by the late, conspicuously unlamented Prinny, and by the present Duke of Sussex.'

'If them, why not him?'

'As I say, it's possible. But remember that Mrs FitzHerbert and Lady Augusta Murray were ladies, were from the sphere of society from which in earlier centuries queens had sometimes come. If Catherine Parr or Elizabeth Woodville, why not Mrs FitzHerbert? But that argument could not apply with Mrs Jordan. She was an actress. Nothing could have made her suitable to be a queen . . .' He pulled himself up short, with the belated sensitivity of the typical aristocrat. 'Do I pain you?'

'No, no. But such a charming woman.'

'Allowed. My young blood was warmed by her beauty and her charm. But she had had protectors before the Duke, had no right that anyone knew of to call herself Mrs and she had had children before his. Another point: she had not stuck out for marriage before. Do you think, because he was a Royal Duke, she would insist on an empty form of marriage?'

I thought.

'No. I did not know her well, but she never struck me as the sort of woman who would do that.'

'As charming off stage as on, Mr Mozart?'

'Fully as charming,' I said, remembering. 'My good friend da Ponte certainly thought so.'

'Promiscuous, Mr Mozart?'

'Generous, My Lord. I would prefer to say generous.'

I thought it politic at that point to let the subject drop. Lord Melbourne was casting too many glances at me instinct with the sharp political intelligence which his lazy manner tried to conceal.

I had a little conversation with my other neighbour, Lord Erroll, who was having noisy exchanges with other guests on the subject of horses (likely winners and the proper management of), hunting, women and dice. Not my sort of person at all. A brash, good-natured, blundering sort of man. The sort who comes to the theatre mainly to observe an actress's ankle. He did condescend over sorbets to ask if I had enjoyed the picnic.

'Very much,' I said. 'Though I don't enjoy the open air as much as I suspect the King does.'

'Oh, he loves it. The whole family does. They were brought up playing games in the grounds of Bushey.'

132

'His Majesty's oldest son didn't seem to be enjoying it.'

'George?' said Erroll, but seeming mentally to back away. 'Gets some funny notions. Finest chap in the world, great company, but gets some funny notions. Feels his position.'

'I can understand that,' I said at once, to stop him turning away. 'I had some conversation with him on the terrace last night. He was ... perhaps not quite himself. He was asking why the King waited so long after parting from Mrs Jordan before he married the present Queen.'

He looked me straight in the eye.

'Gets some odd ideas, George.'

Then he turned determinedly back to his horsy friends. But our conversation had been overheard. Some time later Lord Melbourne bent his head towards me confidentially.

'The reason the King did not marry the Queen until some years after leaving Mrs Jordan is that he tried to marry all sorts of heiresses, to retrieve his financial position. Most of them were almost as unsuitable, as matches, as Mrs Jordan would have been. All of them refused him. He was not a good prospect at all, then. He came to realise that the only chance he had at all of a legal marriage was with a German princess past her first youth. By the time Princess Charlotte died the Continent was again open to English travellers, so he started looking in Germany. Even there it took time.' He smiled wickedly, then wagged his head sagely. 'That I *am* old enough to remember.'

I nodded. It was clear that the time gap between the King's split with Mrs Jordan and his marriage was of no great significance, whatever someone had convinced George FitzClarence was the case. Lord Melbourne now straightened up, looking around benignly as if hoping no one had noticed he had been in a conspiratorial huddle (how naive politicians can be!) and said conversationally: 'Are you still composing, Mr Mozart?'

'I am, My Lord. I have just finished a violin concerto for Paganini. Trying to prevent him writing any more himself.'

When the ladies withdrew Lord Melbourne gave the port five minutes and then went after them. I slipped out in his wake, not to join the ladies (pleasant though that usually is – the beery dreariness of all-male company, whether in taverns or at great tables, always appalls me) but to pursue my investigations. I had been so wrapped up in George FitzClarence that I had neglected other matters. I stopped by the Unfrocked Bishop, who was freezing the area around the staircase.

'I need to talk to Mrs Hattersley, the Princess Victoria's maid.'

I had to repress the desire to say 'My Lord'. Anything to do with the domestic staff was clearly beneath his purview. He raised a finger to summon a lesser footman by the door to the Drawing Rooms, had low words with him, then resumed his episcopal immobility, the only sign of life being the occasional throbbing of the third chin.

The younger footman returned, coming all the way down-stairs, bowing, then leading me up them again (it would have been more than his job – or his life – was worth, I supposed, to shout down to me). He explained when out of earshot of his superior that Mrs Hattersley was in the bedroom of the Princess and her mother, waiting for the Duchess to leave the glittering throng and come to bed. The Princess while at Windsor, as apparently at Kensington too, was on no account to be left alone. She was, however, fast asleep, and Mrs Hattersley could very easily talk to me without fear of being overheard. He led me along the corridor where I had already guessed the Princess and her mother were lodged, and then very quietly opened a heavy door. I slipped through, but as the footman shut it behind me, with the cantankerousness of old buildings, the door creaked.

I was in a very large room, and I could just discern the gloomy shapes of two enormous four-poster beds. In a far corner there was a table, with a candle glimmering on it the sole source of light in the room. There were chairs around it, and Mrs Hattersley had risen out of one, and was beckoning me over: she was hardly more than a gloomy, threatening shape, but as I drew nearer she assumed a less melodramatic aspect.

'The lassie's fast asleep,' she said, gesturing towards the bed nearest the door which held the Princess in its commodious embrace. 'We can talk hearr without fearr.'

I sat down and, keeping my voice low, began business at once.

'You have kept quiet, I hope, about what you saw and heard last night?'

'*I have!*'

I saw a shadow cross her eyes, though.

'But there has been talk among the servants?'

'The sairvants were involved. The sairvants had to remove the body. We are only human. There has been talk.'

'You haven't told the Princess?'

'I have *not*,' she said indignantly, eyeing me through the gloom. 'Why disturb the puir wee child?'

'But very often you do tell her things – things that she otherwise would not know of?'

She shrugged.

'Aye, now and then. For her ain good. They're trying to keep her a child. But she's no a child any longer, and there's things she needs to know.'

'I agree. Is there any talk in the servants' hall about *how* Popper came to meet his death?'

'Naturally there is. If sairvants are commanded to get rid of a corrpse, they'll ask themselves how it came to be a corrpse in the fairst place. But I've said nothing, and Smithson – that's the footman – has said nothing.'

'So the servants' talk is all speculation?'

'Aye, if you like to call it that. There's no solid information, except about what happened to the body at the end.'

'Oh? What did happen?'

'It was taken to his home in London, where the men from here had a tairrible tairmagent to deal with.'

'I know her.'

'Then you're unlucky in your acquaintance, Mr Mozart. They had money, but the body would na' co-operate without she was promised much, much more. In the end she got what she wanted, and the funeral's tomorrow.'

'I see ... Mrs Hattersley, what relation are you to the Hattersley the late Duke of Kent had flogged to death while he was in command in Gibraltar?'

There was a moment's silence. I had no idea what the answer was going to be, but I wondered whether she would say 'husband'. Eventually she said, 'Related by marriage.'

135

'He was not your husband?'

She drew herself up.

'Mr Mozart, how old do you think I am? The things that you're talking about, they happened thairty years ago. I was not even married to John Hattersley at the time.'

Dear, dear – how touchy women are about their age!

'I apologise. I did not know when it happened.'

'And he died after punishment – about a week later.'

'As far as he was concerned that seems to make things worse rather than better.'

'Weel, mebbe you're right. 'Twas often said the Duke was brutal in his punishments.'

'No, the British army is brutal. The Duke was barbaric, from all I've heard.'

'Whatever you say, sir.'

She was being very cagey on the subject, much less than her usual rather theatrical self. It seemed more than the habitual discretion of a royal servant. What, I wondered, was she hiding?

'You bear no resentment for his death?'

'I never knew the man. I only know what my husband told me, which was no' much.'

'What exactly did he tell you?'

She paused, perhaps merely collecting her thoughts and memories, perhaps arranging them for my benefit.

'You must know, sir, that royal sairvice often goes by families. Fathers and mothers get their children places, and their brothers and sisters too if they can, because it's no' bad wages, for all they're not always paid on time. And you can always go on from there to an even better place. My mother worked at Holyrood and got me a place there – and a good place it was, for all there was no royal pairsonage there to serve. My husband was valet to the late Duke of York, and he came to Scotland when he was Commander-in-Chief. We met and married, and we were both in the sairvice of the Duke until first my husband died, then the puir old Duke himself. After that I was fortunate enough to get my present position with the Prrrincess.'

'I see.'

'Matt Hattersley was my husband's uncle. He tried the royal sairvice, but it didn't answer. He was unco' wild, undisciplined, and took a drap too much. He sailed close to the wind, that's how my John put it. When he got dismissed he enlisted for a soldier. It was the last thing such a body should have done. If he could na' take orrders in a royal household, he'd never take orrders for his commanding officers. He couldn't – with the consequences that you know of, sir.'

I meditated for a while. It seemed straightforward enough, and, as far as Mrs Hattersley was concerned, innocent. The idea of her revenging her kinsman's death could surely be set aside. But I still had the distinct feeling that the woman was holding something back, and I saw I had to worry out what it was.

'Which royal household was his service in?' I asked.

'It was the Duke of Cumberland's, sir,' she said.

The Duke again! Would we never be free of the Duke?

'And what was he dismissed for?'

There was silence.

'I'd rather not say.'

'Come, come, Mrs Hattersley. Nothing you can say could harm him now.'

'It's no' him I'm afraid of harming.'

'Mrs Hattersley, I am trying to discover if there is any danger to your young mistress. You will have heard of the incident involving the Duke of Cumberland on the terraces yesterday. Would you really wish to put obstacles of any kind in my way?'

She dabbed her eyes, very distressed at the suggestion.

'No, sir, no! I would na'. It's the last thing I would do . . . Matt was dismissed for spreading malicious rumours, sir.'

'I see. And what or whom did those rumours concern?'

She swallowed.

'They concerned puir Prrincess Sophia.'

Suddenly a long-dead memory, the recollection of long-ago gossip, sprang to my mind. How royal gossip does linger in the back of the mind! It was a story that had had great currency at the time, though it had been generally discounted since.

'Did he spread the rumour that the Duke of Cumberland was the father of his sister's child?'

137

She looked down into her lap.

'Aye, sir, he did, to his shame. Wicked, worrthless crreature that he was. There was no truth in it, that I am quite sure of, Mr Mozart. Not a drop of trruth at all.'

But then how, working at the Palace of Holyrood at the time, would she have known?

There was, I judged, nothing more to be got out of her for the moment. I got up and tiptoed to the door. The bed closest to it was clearer now that my eyes were accustomed to the gloom, and my heart warmed as I discerned the tiny, motionless shape in the middle of its vastness.

Back in the Crimson Drawing Room, now filled with chattering men as well as women, my entry was noted by the Duchess of Kent, who sailed over in my direction, followed – rather reluctantly, it seemed – by Sir John Conroy.

'Mr Mozart, the Duke of Cambridge has just told me a most extraordinary thing.'

I bowed.

'Really? Your Royal Highness?'

'He says that the King has asked to the castle the ... the offspring of Princess Sophia. That he was here all yesterday.'

'Yes, Ma'am, that is true.'

'But that is monstrous! And it goes entirely against the spirit if not the letter of our agreement with the King.'

She looked round at Sir John, who was beginning to look very embarrassed. That 'our' had not been judicious.

'I believe, Ma'am,' I said, 'it was just the kindness of the King's heart. He thought mother and son should get to know each other better.'

'It doesn't seem like kindness at all to me! I think he was being cruel to Sophia.'

'Surely not.'

'Exposing her in that way, publicly.'

'I assure you she herself does not think so.'

She shot me a shocked look.

'You have talked to her abou it?'

'Yes, indeed. I believe the two found very little in common, which was perhaps natural. But she thought it a kind gesture on the King's part.'

Her look said, as clearly as if she had carved it in stone, that she found it astonishing that a mere musician should be discussing intimate and scandalous details of her past with the daughter of a king. A month ago I would have agreed. 'And thus the whirligig of Time brings in his revenges', as the only creative mind comparable to my own once wrote. Maybe my last years would see a mingling with the Great Ones of this world just as my early ones did.

'Well,' said the Duchess briskly, 'it is too late to do anything about it now.' Sir John looked relieved. 'The Princess is asleep, and we leave in any case tomorrow afternoon. But we must watch her – we must all watch her, Mr Mozart. I rely on you.'

Most certainly I would watch her. But I was starting to feel that I could have a longer view than that: I had the faintest glimmer of a hope that I could not only ensure the Princess's safety *now*, but that I could discover who it was who posed the threat to her safety in the future. It would be up to others to put an end to that threat.

FIFTEEN
King and Son

Breakfasts at the castle had been relatively informal during the stay of us visitors. There was a good deal of fend-for-yourself, even though the King or Queen was always there. (The King, by the way, breakfasted remarkably frugally, when one recalled the gargantuan excesses at every possible meal of his late brother.) When, on the last morning of the party, I saw that the Queen was without her husband at breakfast I sent a message, feeling greatly daring, asking if the King could spare me a few minutes alone. The footman's reply was to lead me frostily through to the private apartments of the castle, to the new King's study, a warm, smallish room full (as studies usually are) of books that no one in their senses would want to read.

The King himself was sitting at a desk, with a pile of formal-looking papers beside him to his right, and a bowl of steaming water and a footman to his left. He swivelled round as I was shown into the study.

'Ah, Mr Mozart. Don't bother with the bowing and scraping. Can't do with all that. Give me one "Your Majesty" and then we'll talk man to man, eh?'

'Very well, Your Majesty—'

'Right, that's done. Gets in the way and slows things down, all that nonsense. Sorry to have to go on with this signing. M'brother left a great mountain of stuff – he was sick, of course, at the end, but truth to tell he was never very good at getting the day-to-day things done. Good at the formal stuff, standing around and looking king-like, bad at sticking to the paperwork. Time for a change. I look like the funny old buffer I am, but I'll do the work. Luckily these are just army commissions, so I don't need to read 'em.' He held up a very puffy-looking hand. 'But it still takes it out of me, all this writing.'

The footman bent over and sponged his right hand while with his left the King gestured to a seat beside the desk.

'Well, how are things going, eh? Ready to have anybody keelhauled? Or was it just a storm in a teacup?'

'Not that, Your – sir.' The old man's face fell. 'Mr Nussey feels certain Popper died from poison. That being so, we can't rule out the possibility that the poison was meant for the Princess.'

The King looked up and screwed up his face.

'Not a very likeable little man, was he? That was my impression. Wouldn't have trusted him with a sixpence. May have had lots of enemies. Then again, one of the actresses told me that the Queens Theatre is in a pretty parlous state financially. May have decided to end it all.'

That was a suggestion I had to squash at once.

'If the financial problems of the theatre bothered him he could have committed suicide any time in the last thirty years. He sailed through financial crises like a knife through butter. And he wouldn't have done it now. He was in his seventh heaven at his company's being asked to perform at Windsor, before the new King and Queen. He was politer to me than he had been these ten years.'

The King, signing away, chuckled appreciatively.

'Damned funny people, these theatre managers. Knew Sheridan, y'know. Damned difficult chap. Damned rude too, when he felt like it.'

'Similarly,' I resumed, 'the people who owed him a grudge wouldn't choose to kill him at Windsor, where it was likely to cause the maximum of fuss. If someone drops down dead at a royal reception then questions are bound to be asked about the security around the King and the other royal personages. As far as the theatre people are concerned, Windsor Castle is the last place we would choose if we wanted to murder him. Much though most of us wanted to, from time to time.'

The King put down his pen, and let the footman sponge his swollen hands, before resuming work.

'Adelaide usually does this,' he said complacently. 'Very

gentle. I'm trying to do a year's work in a month, that's the trouble. So then, Mr Mozart, what has been going on?'

'Something I've not got to the bottom of yet, not by a long chalk. I get a whiff – if I may use the word—'

'Certainly you may. I know a stink when I smell one, as I'm sure you do.'

'I get a whiff, then, of some kind of conspiracy. So that what one is after is not necessarily or not only the immediate culprit, but the person or people who lie behind the things that have happened. Do I make myself clear, sir?'

'Clear as an Act of Parliament,' grumbled the King. 'Do you mean that someone is being used, for wicked purposes, by someone else?'

'Probably.'

'Without really understanding what's going on?'

'Again, probably.' (This, by the way, I was far from clear about, but I was already preparing the way for the King to be let down lightly.) 'I wonder, sir, if I could ask you a few questions about personal matters?'

'Not about m'sisters, is it?' he said warily. 'Sad stories. Don't want to bring them in if it can be helped.'

'I mean about yourself, sir.'

'Oh, my life's an open book. Not a very edifying one, a preacher might say, but everyone knows about it.' He scratched his head. 'No one's been very interested in it before. Now everyone's talking about it, and I've forgotten all the details. So don't expect too much of me, Mr Mozart.'

'It was your relationship with Mrs Jordan I was going to ask about.'

'I thought so. Lovely woman.'

'Lovely.'

'Much better than I deserved.'

I was glad he had that much self-knowledge.

'I wondered, sir, whether you ever tried to regularise the union?'

'Regularise? Make it legal?'

'Yes, sir. Go through a ceremony of marriage.'

He gaped at me. Clearly the idea had never occurred to him. 'What would have been the point? That wouldn't have made it legal. The marriage would immediately have been declared invalid by the King m'father.'

'I wondered, sir, if Mrs Jordan might have felt better about the relationship if you had at least tried to make it a formal marriage.'

The King chuckled, and held up his hand to be sponged.

'Not a bit of it. She was an actress, and a realist. She knew the way the world wags. Any marriage would have been a form, a sham. Don't like shams. Like things honest and above board. So did she. Anyway, there was another thing.'

'Yes, sir?'

'Don't know how to put this. Don't want to sound too uppity. Dora was an actress. Even without the damned Royal Marriages Act she wasn't the sort of person a king's son could marry. She'd got three children already, for a start. I knew it wasn't possible, so did she. Actresses could be royal mistresses – remember Nell Gwyn – but they couldn't be royal wives.'

I was glad to have Lord Melbourne's view confirmed.

'So you never went through any ceremony of marriage with her?'

'Never.'

'And any supposed certificate of marriage between you must be a fake?'

'Certainly it must.' The King paused in his writing. 'Mind you, in a way I regarded myself as married to her. Tried to do my best for her, when our ways parted – not that I had much to share with her . . .'

'May I ask why you and she separated, sir?'

He waved the footman away, put down his pen, and looked straight at me.

'Because I was a bounder. And a fool too. I had – what is it that black chappie says in the play? – a pearl of great price, and I let it slip through m'fingers. Oh, there were reasons. Dora and I loved Bushey, and I was always making improvements – in the house, the stables, the grounds. Kept me busy. Didn't have a proper job. Should have had a ship of my own, but m'father stopped me getting one. But it all cost money. I hated to look into the eyes of the workmen and tradesmen that hadn't been paid – horrible! Then all the children – I love them all, but they cost money too. Nobody ever taught me about money when I was growing up. Don't know if I'd have learnt, mind, but nobody tried to teach me. I was in debt before I reached my majority, then deeper and deeper in. I knew I had to do something for my children – King's grandchildren and all that. Couldn't let them go begging, or go on the stage. So I thought the only thing I could do was marry someone with money. Set us all up for life. And Dora too, if I could manage it. She wasn't getting any younger. She'd no more idea about money than I had. Mucked it all up, of course. Lost Dora and never found a rich wife. Served me right for acting like a bounder.'

He turned back to his commissions, and wiped away a tear. Then he motioned the footman back into place and went on signing.

'So your children are still unprovided for?'

'Girls are all right. Married well. Had their mother's looks and charm. Good job they didn't have their father's looks and charm, eh? Boys have had to be found professions – army, navy, church, that kind of thing. Not bad for them, having something to do. But not what I planned. Be easier now, with more nice little things in my gift.'

'You certainly found them all an excellent stepmother.'

'I did, didn't I?' he said, looking up smiling again, very pleased with himself, as always when the Queen was mentioned. 'Excellent woman. Everything a woman should be. Not like m'brother Ernest. Married a woman who murdered her first husband, or so they say. Bet she'd like to murder Ernest now. Everybody else does, anyway. No, I made a good choice. Or, to be honest with you, I was lucky. Because I got engaged to her before I even saw her.'

'Your children get on well with her, it seems.'

'They do. They bully her – but they've got more animal spirits than Adelaide has. Anyway, they bully me too.'

'Your eldest son does not seem happy with his position.'

He shot me a glance. It was a sort of warning.

'George will have to shake down into it. Nothing else he can do, is there? It's not the best thing in the world, being a bastard. But being the King's bastard isn't the worst thing in the world either, eh? Eh?'

144

I stood up, bowed, and the King brushed aside the 'scraping' and waved his pen at me.

'Keep me informed, eh? Me or the Queen. What she knows I know. Trust her on anything except politics. Not for the womenfolk, politics. Keep at it, eh, Mr Mozart? Find out the truth in the end. Got to keep the little girl safe.'

And he turned back to promoting his officers.

In the State Rooms of the castle there was little sign that the house party was coming to an end. Of course there were few (apart from myself) among the guests who had to do anything so mundane as packing. I ascertained that the Princess Victoria was well chaperoned (watched over by Lehzen she was teaching one of the Erroll children to pick out a tune on the old fortepiano in the King's Closet, and she was much bossier than I ever was as a music teacher), and having satisfied myself about that I went in search of my next prey. Fortunately the Countess of Erroll was on her own, walking thoughtfully in the Quadrangle. She smiled as I came up to her, but it was a troubled smile, as if I represented part of the problem she was in the process of thinking through.

'Lady Erroll, I wonder if I could ask you about something you said during the picnic yesterday.'

'Ah . . .'

'You seemed to be saying it not so much to yourself as to me, to get a message across to me.'

This time her smile had something teasing and even coquettish about it.

'Well, you are, are you not, Mr Mozart, doing something confidential for Papa? That is clear to everyone here. And you are also keeping an eye on little Victoria.'

'There are many of us doing that, though too often we nod off. I'm sure you remember what you said, Lady Erroll: "Sometimes I worry about George."'

'I remember . . . You are quite right, Mr Mozart: I was not talking to myself. I have been worried about George for some time now. I've been walking here wondering whether to talk to someone – to you, to Papa, to the Lord Chamberlain.'

'I hope you will decide to talk to me.'

'You give me little choice. I shall have to say something now.

In any case it will be a relief . . .' She thought for some time, obviously approaching a difficult subject with care. 'We're a harum-scarum, healthy, selfish, fairly happy lot, Mr Mozart – I mean my brothers and sisters and I. "The FitzClarences" as people call us, as if we were all alike, and a sort of family firm. Or else a nasty illness, depending on your point of view. But George is the exception. He's not at all harum-scarum, not at all happy. I don't know – perhaps it's because he's the eldest . . . I do notice that you've had your eyes on him, Mr Mozart.'

'I'm trying to avoid trouble for the King.'

'I'm afraid George *is* trouble for the King.'

'I rather thought he was. What do you think his problem is?'

'I think he is losing his grip on reality – *our* reality. He has been babbling on to me about a marriage certificate.'

I nodded.

'Yes, he was talking to me the other night about why the King had not married the Queen until 1818. I concluded he meant until after your mother had died.'

'I expect he did. He's got the idea that Papa and Mama went though some kind of marriage ceremony. Such nonsense! Even if they did, it would not have been legal, because Grandpapa King (we were always brought up to call him that) had not given his consent. And in that case, what difference would it make? I would hope that people could accept us for what we are, not because of some scrap of paper our parents obtained.'

'Your father says there never was any such marriage.'

'There you are. But I never thought there was.'

'On my first night here I heard your brother asking the King to make him Prince of Wales.'

'Oh my God!' She turned and looked at me, consternation on her face. 'Was he drunk?'

'Rather, yes. But—'

'But it seemed to be a genuine demand.' She looked down in thought, then we resumed our walk round the Quadrangle. 'It's worse than I realised, isn't it? George is going off into some sort of fantasy world. Is he mad yet, do you think?'

'I don't know. Do you know how he's got hold of this supposed certificate?'

'There's an actual certificate, is there? I've no idea. If he

146

thinks it's genuine, then there's no question of his having faked it himself, is there?'

'No, that's not what I think. My guess would be that someone has brought it to him, knowing his obsession.'

She nodded her head vigorously, as she did everything.

'I told you, Mr Mozart, that we all had fantasies as children that somehow we would prove to be real princes and princesses. Apparently George never grew out of them – that is something I never realised till now.'

'And apparently someone is using them. That's what I want to find out. Who is using your brother's—' I hesitated.

'Madness.'

'Let's say obsession, Lady Erroll. Who is using his obsession, and what are they trying to make him do?'

Before we parted Lady Erroll promised to tell me anything she could learn from her brother – 'for the King's sake, for the Princess's, and for poor George's own sake,' she said, with an expression unusually worried and concerned.

I was not, however, going to leave further investigation of 'poor George' – mere tool though I felt he was – to the chance that he would spill his soul out to his sister. I therefore made it my business during the rest of the morning to find out where he was. I wandered through the State Rooms, on the terraces, around the rest of the castle, even into the Great Park, to no avail. I saw all the other players in the drama, including Princess Victoria, who was playing a boisterous game of something-or-other with Lord Melbourne and some of the other children, watched over by her mother and Lehzen, both looking jealous, and by Sir John, looking distinctly discontented and ill-tempered: negotiations, I conjectured, were not going his way over the question of who was to control any extra funds that Parliament might vote for the Princess's household.

The footmen knew nothing of George FitzClarence's whereabouts, and the approach of luncheon did not see him joining the company, so I decided to forswear the meal and continue my search. I was finally rewarded by a sighting of him, coming in at the St George's Gate, apparently on his way back from Windsor itself. He was walking somewhat jauntily, and turned down in the direction of the Lower Ward and St George's

Chapel. I went after him with a nonchalance that was partly assumed, partly genuine, for I had very little idea, should I get to talk to him, how I was to approach the topic I had at heart, or what specifically I would ask him.

When I got down to the Lower Ward he was nowhere to be seen. Instead of investigating the medieval shambles of the Horseshoe Cloister I decided to try St George's Chapel. It was a fine day, and entering through the main door I was glad to find it grand but far from gloomy. Its size was not such as to remove it from the human scale, and it provided a setting more homely than might have been expected for the assorted monarchs and their consorts whose graves and monuments were situated there.

It was a minute or two before I saw him. He came out from the far aisle, where it ran the length of the choir, and he stood there near the altar, looking down the length of the nave. He was once again posing – perhaps this time for one of those historical pieces that are becoming so popular: *Henry VII on the Battlefield of Bosworth; Charles II Receiving the Plaudits of his Subjects on his Return to London.* The handsome acquiline nose, the high forehead, the firm mouth – all perfect, and all reminding me of someone: was it someone I had known, or a picture of someone perhaps?

I strolled over.

'A grand place,' I said conversationally. 'Full of the most interesting memorials.'

'The tombs of my forebears,' he said, in a voice instinct with drama. Here was a new role: the Master of Ravenswood in the halls of his ancestors, in one of the novels of Sir Walter that has not yet been made into a bad opera by anybody. It was difficult to think of a suitable response.

'Yes, indeed,' I said idiotically. 'It must be a . . . moving experience for you.'

'I came here before once,' he said, with a rapt intensity that was unnerving. 'I suppose I was about twenty, and it was my father's birthday. The old Queen consented to my being of the party, and she received me. The old bitch! Made me feel like a mongrel cur among pedigrees. She must have had a real gift to be able to do that – ugly as sin herself, and

148

surrounded by a brood most of them as unprepossessing as herself.'

'Queen Charlotte had the reputation of being less than amiable,' I said.

'Much less. But how do you account for that gift – of making her hideous brood seem like pedigrees, while I . . .'

While I, handsome, gallant and talented, was made to feel like a cur, went the unspoken remainder of the sentence.

'The trappings of royalty might do much,' I suggested, 'as well as the knowledge that possession was theirs, not yours.'

'Well, things change, don't they?' he said, his words very distinct, and I smelt brandy on his breath and caught a glint in his eye. 'Circumstances change. One day I may be able to stand here, on her grave, and say "Well, you old bitch, what do you think of the mongrel now?" Oh, I had my fill of her condescension, of her *kindness* – she really did think she was being kind, you know. But one day I'll really crow at her shade!'

'Already you are here – son of the King,' I said.

'Oh, now! Now is nothing!' We had strolled down the nave and now emerged into the sunlight. I could see not just his handsome face but the eyes too, the glint in which was not liveliness or humour, but seemed a light which spoke of obsession, of madness, quite marring the man's beauty. 'Now they talk, now they sneer. Not to our faces, not in the King's presence. But go into the next room and you'll hear them sneer. "The FitzClarences are getting above themselves." "The FitzClarences are making hay while the sun shines." That other German bitch – the widow of Kent – didn't want her daughter to meet us, as if we were pitch which would defile her. Oh, the time will come! I'll show *her* as well!'

'You said the other night—' I began, but he immediately drew himself up, as if surprised, and interrupted me.

'Have I talked to you?'

'Two nights ago. On the terrace.'

He thought.

'Are you one of the theatre people?'

'Wolfgang Gottlieb Mozart. The composer.'

'Hmmm.'

'You said on the terrace that it was significant that your father did not marry the Queen until the year "eighteen".' A shadow crossed his eyes, consciousness that he had been a fool. But he said nothing and I was forced to go on. 'Did you mean that he couldn't marry her until your mother was dead? Or *felt* he couldn't, perhaps?'

There was a long silence. I had clearly lost my prey – I could almost see the deer running away towards the forest.

'My meaning I leave up to you, Mr Mozart. Maybe there was no meaning in my words. I was a little drunk, was I not?'

'*In vino veritas*,' I said inanely.

'Sometimes, Mr Mozart. But sometimes not truth, but a great deal of nonsense, as I'm sure you know. I am a cautious man, Mr Mozart. I take no steps I have not deeply thought out beforetimes. Like my mother: she never took on a new role but she knew it inside out in advance – not just the words, but every movement, every look, every gesture. As to the future, we advance slowly, taking here a field, there a hill, now a village. Caution, Mr Mozart – that is our watchword!'

That from the man who had demanded that his father make him Prince of Wales! I was about to frame some further questions when he swung away from me, and with long strides proceeded along the path around the Lower Ward and up towards the castle. As I watched his upright bearing and striking profile, seemingly made for the coinage, I suddenly remembered who that profile reminded me of. It was my dear old friend da Ponte, best of all collaborators, in the year he arrived in this God-forsaken country, when his only words of English were 'women', 'wine' and 'credit', and when he was utterly besotted by the charms of the actress Dorothea Jordan.

SIXTEEN
Child of Nature

I followed George FitzClarence thoughtfully up to the castle. I was convinced now that he was a man of powerful passions and unstable mind, whose brooding on his supposed wrongs had unsettled him to the point of madness. I say supposed wrongs because, as the King had said, there were worse things than being the natural son of a member of the Royal Family. But such an argument could only be appreciated by a stable mind – by such a one as his sister's, for example – and I was convinced that, from his early years, George FitzClarence had lovingly nursed and nourished his grievance. His comments on the Old Queen, though superficially understandable, had all the hallmarks of an old grudge, mentally mulled over and over until it had become a mania.

But what I needed to know was: who was behind the man's current obsessions and actions? That there was somebody was clear – that person had supplied him with a bogus wedding certificate or transcript of a church register. He was an instigator, not a lieutenant, and he was acting from motives so far unclear. That same person, I was sure, was still busily stoking the fires of the man's obsession. Probably he had been at it that very morning. I remembered that he had come in from the town, and that he had had alcohol on his breath.

When I arrived at the castle I took the unlikely step of asking to speak privately with Lord Howe, the Queen's Chamberlain. I knew I was not merely *persona non grata* to him, but practically non-existent in a worldly sense. I had conceived what could optimistically be called a plan of action, and the only person I could think of who might have the sort of personality necessary to bring it off was that cold, rigid, forbidding man. From the fact that he scared me I drew the inference that he might scare others. He received me in his magnificent but chilly office (if such it might be called) deep in the bowels of the castle.

'Lord Howe, I am sorry to disturb you,' I opened, 'but I am afraid I am in need of assistance.' There was the slightest of nods, indicative of the fact that he was accustomed to demand service rather than have it demanded of him. Particularly by a jobbing musician. Indeed, for all I knew he may have thought I was about to demand assistance of a pecuniary nature. Particularly if he knew my reputation. I hastened on. 'As you are aware, My Lord, the King has asked me to enquire into . . . into a most delicate matter, which may shortly come to a . . . to a climax, perhaps a resolution.'

'Good,' he enunciated, very tight-lipped.

'To achieve this resolution, it may be necessary to use all the authority, the weight, of the Crown. Without, if that is possible, directly involving the King or Queen.'

He thought about this for some time.

'I see,' he said at last, with the tiniest diminution of chill. 'It is always best not to involve the Sovereign directly. That has always been my policy and practice. The purpose of a royal servant such as myself is to deflect criticism, to keep royal personages above vulgar argument. But is there – ' there was a sharp intake of breath, suggesting a distaste at having to ask for information from so manifestly inferior a being – 'any additional reason for keeping Their Majesties at some distance in so far as concerns the resolution of this matter?'

He was sharper than I had thought.

'It is a question of the King's natural affections,' I said. He remembered our earlier conversation and saw the point at once.

'I see. Go on.'

'I need Your Lordship's help in two ways. The first may seem small, but I feel Your Lordship's authority within the castle may lead to success more quickly than any enquiry of my own could. I need to know where the man called Tom Garth or Captain Garth drinks, and if possible where he lodges, and I think the best way to find that out is to enquire from the footmen and

152

the domestic staff here at the castle. In their off-duty hours they probably frequent the inns and taverns of Windsor.'

He looked as if I had asked him to empty a privy, but after a moment's thought he rang a little bell. The footman who came in was tall and young, and looked so like a young scion of the aristocracy that I wondered about his intelligence. However when Lord Howe, in a voice swimming with distaste, had succinctly set out what was required of him, the man nodded as if such things were all in a day's work, and bowed himself out to set about it. Lord Howe turned back to me.

'You mentioned two ways . . . ?'

'Yes. The second is that I would ask you, respectfully, to hold yourself in readiness, My Lord. I may have to ask you to represent what I called the authority of the Crown against this man Garth. It may be necessary to cow him to silence, it may be necessary to force him to leave the country. If all else fails, the authority of the Crown might be obliged to bribe the whole story out of him.'

He nodded almost complacently.

'I have been involved in such duties from time to time. Before I became Chamberlain to Her present Majesty, of course. Such exercises of royal authority are usually successful. The Crown *has* powers, even in this levelling age, and I am always happy to exercise them. There is in this case a complicating factor—'

I took his point at once.

'Quite, My Lord. The man seems quite willing to use his . . . supposed origins. However, we will hope to find some way of rendering that factor useless to him.'

His expression suggested he had had a chamber-pot emptied over him from an upstairs window.

'Any more public comment on the matter would be most regrettable.'

'True, My Lord. But we must use what weapons we can. The main purpose of our efforts must surely be to protect the Princess Victoria.' This time he nodded with a frozen kind of enthusiasm. 'Then Your Lordship will hold yourself in readiness?'

He bowed almost imperceptibly, and waited for me to depart.

When I had completed the trek back to the State Apartments luncheon was over and some of the castle guests were lounging about or pursuing their usual occupations of cards or billiards, while others seemed to be preparing for departure. I looked for the Princess Victoria, but since she was not to be found, nor any of her party, I presumed she was one of the latter group – her mother making her escape as early as possible with a sigh of relief, no doubt. I was just wondering what to do with myself when I was approached by the aristocratic young sprig of a footman, who had gone about the tasks set him most expeditiously.

'Mr Mozart? I've got the information you require.'

'Splendid.'

'The man Garth mostly tipples at the Five 'Orseshoes, or failing that the Fox and Newt or the Duke of Marlborough. The general opinion is that he's a dodgy cove.'

'I suspect that the general opinion is correct.'

'We're not so sure about 'is lodgings, but someone has 'eard 'im mention Mrs Lupton's in Washing Alley. Lets rooms with meals as required to gentlemen, but not too gentlemanly ones, if you take my meaning.'

'I do. I am very grateful to you.'

'Take care, Mr Mozart. We don't want anything 'appening to you so there's no more jolly music, do we?'

His heart seemed to be in the right place, and he showed a welcome element of warmth in that chilly environment, so I thanked him heartily. I immediately set out for the St George's Gate and the picturesque if dirty town of Windsor. I was not well acquainted with the place, but it is not large and I immediately set off in quest of the various hostelries the young man had mentioned. The Five Horseshoes I found easily – a large, bustling place built in my lifetime, but though I searched through its many rooms and snugs clutching a glass of gin and water for which I had very little use I could find no sign of Tom Garth. The Duke of Marlborough hardly measured up to the greatness of its namesake, being a tumbledown hovel from the Duke's own time, but again there was no Tom Garth. However, when I spotted the Fox and Newt down a dull, dark lane I somehow knew I would find my man there, and I was right. He was down the far end of the bar, lounging against it with the ease of long familiarity, and surrounded by a little knot of cronies.

'A bottle of your finest sherry, landlord,' I said grandly, and took myself to a table in their vicinity.

The men surrounding my quarry were a raffish-looking lot. Their clothes had once been good – probably when worn by someone else – but were now ill-fitting and far from clean. Some of their faces had not seen a razor in the last two or three days, and probably not even a face-cloth either. They smelt of sweat, tobacco and the stables, and several of them, Tom Garth included, were smoking long, curly pipes. Their talk was of horses and dogs – not so very different from Lord Errol's conversation as far as the subject-matter was concerned, but decidedly different as to the tone. These men were *low*, and Tom Garth was diving down to meet them.

I had to wait quite a while, and was well into my third glass of sherry, before the conversation turned away from the equine and the canine.

'If you're going to stake ten guineas on Morning Glory,' said one of these rough rakes to Tom Garth, 'then your fortunes are looking up.'

Tom Garth looked pleased with himself, and tapped the side of his nose.

'Maybe so, old cock, maybe so. The state of the pocket-book is looking distinctly healthy.'

'Your distinguished family doing the decent thing?'

Tom Garth puffed out his cheeks in disgust.

'My distinguished family doesn't want to know me. My distinguished family would very much rather I had never come into the world to embarrass their greatness with my very existence. Incumbrances born to men are one thing – particularly when the men reach what you might call the top of their profession. Incumbrances born to young ladies are quite another thing.'

'There you're being unfair, Tom,' said another of them, in whom some flicker of the flame of loyalty seemed to burn. 'The new head of the family seems a jolly old cove enough, and he invites you to the family 'ome. That you

155

told us. You can't say the family don't want to know you, can you?'

'By "know" I mean do the generous thing, Jim,' said Tom Garth, whose priorities, I had to admit, were not a hundred miles removed from my own. 'Do the *decent* thing, come to that. Invitations are cheap and butter no parsnips. No, if I have a few guineas to lay on a decent prospect in the horseflesh line it has been gained by the sweat of my brow.'

The talk, infuriatingly, now turned back to the turf. I meditated on Tom Garth's accent, which was much better than the rest's. He had the tones and grammar of an educated man. But they had slipped towards roughness, as if men of this type were the ones he nowadays most usually associated with. No wonder he had looked uneasy and out of place at the castle.

I ordered a slice of goose pie with the usual trimmings and settled in for a long wait. I was on my fifth glass before the talk turned back to a topic of any interest to me. It was provoked by someone shaking his head and saying regretfully, 'You've got to have the contacts.'

'Too true, my boy,' said Tom Garth. 'You've got to have the contacts – both up and down.'

'What do you mean, up and down?'

'My philosophy of life,' said Garth expansively, 'gained from bitter experience, is never to be the initiator.'

'The what?'

'Never be the one who sets a nice little scheme in motion,' the man explained, expansively. 'That way if things go wrong it's you who ends up carrying the can. I've tried that, and nearly came a frightful cropper. I could have not only carried the can but ended up in jug, like as not. No, the best trick is to make yourself useful to somebody. That way there's someone there to shuffle the blame on to. As to *down*, well, my plan is always to employ professionals.'

'Experts, like?'

'Experts, Sam. People who really know what they're doing. Take a case in point. Say, just for the sake of argument I wanted a letter written in someone's else's hand. Or say I wanted an official-looking form. Now, I could make a fist at things of that kind myself, no question. But would they stand up to close scrutiny?'

'Not these days,' said Sam sagely. 'The authorities have become powerful sharp.'

'They have,' agreed Tom Garth. 'More's the pity. So if you want a job done, you go looking for the best man for the job – an expert imitator of the autography of other people.' His audience nodded, but in a bemused way, as if unused to words of more than two syllables. 'And when I find him, I give him exact and precise directions as to what he should do. I tell him *what* to do, but I don't tell him *why* he's doing it. Not his business, see? And when the job is done I pay him generously – or my principal does – and that is the end of the matter. Unless it were to happen that I should need him again, in which case I know where to go.'

'Very wise,' they collectively murmured. 'That's the way to go about things. Stands to reason.'

'Likewise, if I wanted to nobble a horse – which God forbid, having too much respect for the noble beasts – ' he drew in a mouthful of smoke from his pipe and let it out in a satirical spiral, to appreciative chuckles from his audience – 'I would never attempt to do the job myself, unless I fancied having my skull crushed by a hoof. I would find a man who'd done it before, and was willing to do it again with no questions asked. And when he'd done the job I'd pay him well. Generosity is the watchword in these dealings, if you don't want falling-out among . . . gentlemen. My distinguished family once tried to buy me off. They didn't do it . . . wholeheartedly enough. They may live to regret it.'

He took from the pocket of his waistcoat a gold watch.

'Fine ticker, Tom,' said the man he called Sam.

'Present from my . . . my father, on my going into the army. Not a profession for a man of independent ideas, Sam. That was my experience, anyway. No doubt the Duke of Wellington would disagree – one of my fellow-guests at the castle, though we didn't manage to exchange ideas.' He winked – the bar-room card. 'Well, I must be off. Mother Lupton's dinner-hour approaches, so my watch and my internal organisation tell me. With regret, my friends – ' he took his pipe

157

from his mouth and gave a parody of a bow – 'I must bid you good day.'

And he took himself off towards the door. I had already put down my knife and fork over the half-eaten goose pie (as so often happens the goose seemed to have led a too long and too active life to be comfortable eating). I swilled down the sherry in my glass, leaving the dregs in the bottle, and got up in an unhurried way and followed him out of the Fox and Newt.

When I emerged into the dreary lane it was situated in he was not to be seen, but once back at the road I saw he was taking the direction away from the castle. I could not follow him too fast – my years did not permit that, and in any case I had no intention of drawing his notice to me. He walked on quite unsuspiciously for two or three minutes, then turned into another mean side lane. When I reached it I saw it was Washing Alley, and saw a door shutting of a house some yards down it that was really two cottages put together. I paused, wondering what was best to do, and unwilling to lose track of my quarry. There was a small shop opposite advertising 'Pies, Pasties and Fine Pork Sausages, prop. Mrs Beddowes', and when I lounged towards it I saw that in addition to its counter it had two rough benches and tables. It seemed to be my day for pies. I walked in, feeling the incongruousness of my dress and the low pastry shop, and ordered a slice of cold pork pie from the harassed but good-natured woman behind the counter.

'And do you know anybody – a son or daughter, perhaps – who could take a message for me to the castle?'

'I surely do, sir. My son Bob. BOB! Come on here, boy!'

Bob turned out to be a forward-looking boy whose eye glinted with amazed anticipation when I took a shilling from my pocket. I borrowed a pencil and a sheet of rough paper from his mother, and wrote:

My Lord.

I am in Washing Alley, a humble lane off King George Street. The man we wish to talk to is at his dinner in lodgings opposite the pie shop where I am waiting. I would be greatly obliged if Your Lordship could come as expeditiously as possible with two able-bodied footmen, so that, with Your Lordship's assistance, the matter can have a favourable outcome.

I am

Your Lordship's humble servant,
Wolfgang Gottlieb Mozart

I read it over again. It seemed sufficiently obsequious. Then I folded it, gave it to the boy with instructions to deliver it to the officer on the castle gate as a message of the greatest urgency, and set him running off up King George Street to the castle.

I settled down to my pork pie, hoping the pig had led a more sedentary life than the goose.

SEVENTEEN
At Bay

It was a little over half an hour before I was disturbed in my hideyhole over the remains of my pork pie. The friendly young footman appeared outside the window, and when I slipped out I saw a second stalwart figure and, in the shadows, Lord Howe, enveloped in a dark cape. I was glad I could not see his face. He had probably never been before in so low an alleyway. I gestured towards the house I took to be Mrs Lupton's lodging house for gentlemen. We were just approaching the street door when a chirpy voice said, 'You'd best guard the back, misters. They often escapes through the window at the back.'

It was Bob, my bright young messenger. Lord Howe tipped him a penny, and gestured to my friend the footman to take a small, dark path around the house. At the back we saw him vault over a low fence, skirt a tethered goat, and then take up a position under the window. Then, at a gesture from Lord Howe, the other footman went back to the door and banged his fist on it in a manner the castle servants had obviously developed to keep the citizens of Windsor in awe: authoritative it certainly was, though hardly tactful in its implied message that the castle somehow owned Windsor. There was a scurrying of skirts on the other side of the door, and after a minute it was opened by a flabby woman with a streaming red nose and an ineradicable tendency to curtsy to gentlemen.

'Oh, good evening sir, sirs—'

Lord Howe stepped forward.

'We wish to speak to Mr Thomas Garth.'

'Oh, My Lord, I'll see where he is.' (She called him My Lord, not, I suspected, because she knew who he was, but because he

160

was so lordly. I was surprised she didn't call him Your Grace.)
'He finished his dinner a while ago, Mr Garth did. That's his
room at the top of the stairs.'

She seemed to want to avoid another traipsing up to the first
floor, so I and the footman went ahead, and on opening the
door we were just in time to see legs disappearing through
an open window, immediately succeeded by shouts from the
garden below. The footman ran down to give assistance but it
was not needed. Within a couple of minutes Tom Garth was
being press-ganged into his own bedroom, one arm twisted
behind his back in what is popularly known as a half-Nelson
(in tribute, no doubt, to the English national hero, half of
whom would not have made a very impressive figure). Once
he was well into the room, and the door was locked behind
him, the footman flung him into a chair in disgust.

'He's a cheat, that one,' he said. 'Welshed on a bet with a
mate of mine. Don't trust nothin' 'e says.'

He was frozen by a look from Lord Howe. Certainly if his friend
had put his trust in Tom Garth he had misplaced it horribly.
Getting my first good look at him close to, he seemed so obviously
crooked that only the morally dubious were likely to consider
having dealings with him. His dark eyes under beetling brows shot
a look of resentment at the footman, then went on to Lord Howe
and quickly away again. But his discomfiture was short-lived: he
was adept, through practice, at picking himself up, physically and
morally, and after a moment or so he shook himself, sat upright
in his chair, and looked around the assembled company.

'Well now, gentlemen: well and truly caught. Let's get down
to business. Let me hear what you want of me. And then I'll
let you hear what I want of you.'

As a piece of bravado it was breath-taking. It was also rather
well done. I heard a sharp intake of breath from Lord Howe.
I realised I was the only one who had the necessary knowledge
of what he had been up to to take him on, and I decided I had
a tough adversary.

'What we want from you is answers to our questions,' I said,
with an attempt at severity.

'Oh yes? And by what right are you questioning me?' he
asked perkily.

'By order of the King,' I said, stretching the truth.

'Oh yes? Well, the King is a jolly old cove—'

'Show some respect!' hissed Lord Howe, through thin lips.

'Personally I don't know how to show more respect than to say a man is a jolly old cove,' he said, his cheekiness undiminished. 'As I was saying the King is a jolly old gentleman, and he has done very kindly by me in a number of ways, so if he wants the answers to a few questions, then ask away!'

I settled myself down on his bed.

'We want to know first of all about a document purporting to be a record of marriage between the present King, when Duke of Clarence, and Dorothea Jordan, the actress.'

Tom Garth scratched his head theatrically.

'You know, I do seem to have heard talk of some such document. I don't know where. Wait a minute – perhaps it was from George FitzClarence, the King's son. I think it must have been. You'd best go and ask him about it.

'We know already that he has some such document,' I said testily. 'An entirely spurious thing. The question is, how did he get hold of it?'

'Best thing would be to ask him, wouldn't it?' The man sat forward in his chair and sneered at me, and even at Lord Howe. 'Or do you prefer not to, because he is the son of a king? That's interesting! Say we'd gone through all the precious children of King George III and their offspring and we'd come to my mother and she was Queen Sophia, would I get a bit of respect? Would you be a bit chary about having a footman frog-march me up the stairs and throw me into a chair? Well, now, that could be something to look forward to!'

Lord Howe's face wore an expression of pain, that such things could be talked about – and by a son! – in the presence of menials.

'I'm not interested at the moment in the man who has the document,' I said, 'but in the man who provided him with it, even if he didn't actually forge it himself.'

He looked at me closely, his mouth twisted satirically.

'Been listening to private conversations, have we?' he asked. 'I didn't recognise you in the Fox and Newt, but you're the cove who played the piano at the little piece they put on at

162

the castle, aren't you? Bit odd when my uncle the King has to employ a piano strummer to do his dirty work for him. Suggests that things are not quite what they should be.'

'I'd advise you to show some respect,' said Lord Howe in his constipated voice. 'It is not so long since a low scribbler spent two years in Surrey Gaol for libelling the Prince Regent.'

'If you're referring to Mr Hunt,' said Tom Garth imperturbably, 'what he said was that the Regent was a libertine head over ears in debt and disgrace, and that was no more a libel than – all right! All right!' Lord Howe had pushed the stalwart footman forward to menace him and stop his mouth. 'Well, we don't seem to be much forrader, do we? You say that George FitzClarence has a document, and I say I don't know how he got it.'

'I saw you give it to him – yesterday at the picnic,' I said, stretching the truth.

'*Did* you? Were you close enough to see what it was? No, of course you weren't Mr Whatever-your-name is. Nobody was. Next question?'

'I would advise you not to trifle with us,' said Lord Howe, with icy fury. 'The King has powers—'

'Oh, I wouldn't threaten me with the King's powers, if I were you,' said Tom Garth, with an unpleasant laugh. He leaned forward. 'Because I'll tell you this: if I'm accused of anything, George FitzClarence will be accused of worse. If I'm in anything, then I'm up to my ankles, but George FitzClarence is up to his eyes in it. You accuse one and you accuse both.'

'You can be accused of procuring a forgery without involving him,' I suggested, but not hopefully.

'Oh?' The man laughed outright. 'And do you think no questions would be asked as to why that *particular* forgery might be profitable to me? Oh no, Mr—'

'Mozart.'

'Mozart. Funny name. Oh no, if a little comes out, then everything comes out.'

That, in a nutshell, was our problem.

'You are underestimating the King's powers,' Lord Howe said, but it sounded like a last throw. 'You talk about questions being asked, but you could be put away for a very

long time and no one would have a chance to ask questions at all.'

The scoundrel actually laughed in his face.

'Come, come, Lord—'

'Howe,' I supplied, because he couldn't bear to.

'Come, come, Lord Howe. We are living in the nineteenth
century. And let me tell you I have written (damned fag it
was too) an account of the whole matter, detailing everyone's
involvement. A copy of that account will be put into the hands
of the King if anything should happen to me. I am a man with
friends, and one of them will do exactly that. I would advise
you to have done with threats, My Lord.'

'On the other hand, inducements . . . ?' I suggested. He was
delighted and relaxed at once into his chair.

'Right. What did I say when we started? We've heard what you
want of me, but that's the wrong way round: I want to hear what
you'll do for me, and then I'll give you – the arrangements being
satisfactory, of course – an account of the whole matter.'

I turned my head towards Lord Howe.

'Five thousand pounds, on condition that you give us a full
account of the affair, and then leave England, not coming back
for at least ten years.'

Ten years, I'm sure Lord Howe calculated, would see the
present King out of this world. The man was a realist, albeit
of a rather unpleasant kind. Tom Garth gave a show of
considering.

'Ten thousand and it's a deal.'

'Done,' said Lord Howe, who was clearly used to business of
this kind (serving such a family it was perhaps not surprising).
He gestured to one of the footmen, who produced paper of
an impressively official kind. Lord Howe went over to a little
table under the window, and using Tom Garth's pen and ink
wrote five or six lines. He presented them to the scallywag, who
read them through carefully, pondered, and then signed. Lord
Howe folded the paper into the pocket of his dress coat, then
gestured to the footmen to leave the room. I imagined them
outside on the landing, their ears glued to the door. Such a
thought did not occur to Lord Howe. He turned back to the
man in the chair.

'Now,' he said.

Tom Garth scratched his ear.

'Difficult to know where it all started. I suppose the real beginning was when the present King came to the throne, or maybe even a bit before that, because the old King was failing for months, and people were talking about what would happen when the Duke of Clarence became King – laughing about it a bit, too, because the Duke was a bit of a joke. It started going around – among gentlemen in the know, that is – that a certain person who would then be very close to the throne was becoming not quite right in the head on the subject of his own birth.'

'George FitzClarence,' I said. 'There need be no beating about the bush in the privacy of this room.'

'George FitzClarence,' he agreed equably. 'He'd always been a bit unbalanced – that's why his army career, with all his advantages and connections, was a chequered one. Brilliant, handsome, unbalanced – an interesting combination. And as his father approached the throne he was getting to a condition close to madness. The fact that he *was* so close to the throne – not *legally*, but close to the King's affections – suggested the possibility that there might be some rich pickings in prospect.'

'You having already successfully blackmailed your mother,' I put in. He was unperturbed.

'Quite. Only moderately successfully, and done through third parties so she hardly knew anything was going on. Well, what is a bastard child to do, to get the things that ought to be his by rights? Let's stick to the point, shall we? The first thing to be done was to convey to the King's son the idea that there was in existence a letter from the King to Mrs Jordan appointing a time for them to go through a ceremony of marriage. This was the start of our exciting him, stirring up the fever in his blood – which was there, as you well know, long before I did anything about it. Every bastard would prefer to think his parents had gone through some kind of marriage ceremony. I told him I thought I could get hold of it for a fee. I have a very good little chap who is a genius at . . . penmanship. I was the one who told him what to write, of course, and got the specimen of the

King's handwriting. I put together something that I thought could pass muster. "Dearest Dora, the place is St Peter's in Holborn, the time is twelve o'clock on Wednesday 1st April, when we shall be joined in the eyes of heaven at least, if not in my father's. Your ever-loving William." I made him put in a couple of misspellings, to make it convincing, and dated it March 1793, more than a year before his birth. People can be just as sensitive about their conception as about their birth.'

'I can see this would please a natural child,' I said, puzzled, 'particularly one as sensitive as George FitzClarence. But I can't see why a supposed marriage should excite him so much, when it would still be an illegal one.'

Tom Garth laughed.

'*In conjunction.* We had a second card up our sleeves. When you have someone as . . . excitable as George FitzClarence was when his father became King, you can feed him all sorts of stuff and be believed. I started feeding him the notion that people were commenting on the fragile life of little Princess Victoria, which was the only thing that stood to prevent the Duke of Cumberland coming to the throne on his father's death. People were talking, I said, about the end of the monarchy in England, because the people of England would never accept such a man as King. And the fact is, what I said was true: people were talking, and they were saying just that.'

'That may very well be true,' I said. 'I don't think they would accept the Duke of Cumberland as King. But I fail to see how that could affect George FitzClarence in any way. Even if his parents had gone through a form of marriage, it was totally illegal.'

'Ah ha! True enough,' he said, with considerable self-approbation. 'But once I'd planted that idea, I had another up my sleeve to put into his head. I constructed another letter and took it to my little man. This one was in the handwriting of the Duke of Wellington. Very well he did it too. The Duke's gruff little notes are famous, and as an old soldier I had no trouble getting hold of a specimen of his handwriting. Wait a second – I think I have my rough draft. This is the one that *really* excited him!'

He got up and rummaged among the papers on his desk,

finally coming up with a sheet which he handed to Lord Howe. I went across and read it over his shoulder.

To the Rt Hon. Sir Robert Peel.

My dear Peel,

I write to convey my thoughts on the subject we touched on at the Mansion House banquet. The prospect of the Duke of Cumberland as King is one the British nation would never accept. It would spell a certain Republic. To cut him out of the succession, with his son, would be to leave the Duke of Sussex as heir – a mad radical, and as *mad* as he is *radical.* I favour the solution of repealing the Royal Marriages Act (which should never have been enacted) and declaring valid all marriages in the royal family contracted in defiance of it since. This would have the virtue of being an Act of Justice, and would appeal to the public's sense of fairness.

Yours,
Wellington.

'But this is preposterous!' protested Lord Howe. 'A Tory prime minister would never contemplate barring anybody from the succession to the throne! The Tory party is the party of loyalty.'

'Are they, My Lord?' said Garth, with a sneer on his face. 'They transferred their loyalty from the Stuarts to the Hanoverians when they realised they were never going to come to power on the coat-tails of the Old or the Young Pretenders. *Not* so preposterous, My Lord. And certainly not preposterous to one who *wants* to believe it, and is on the verge of insanity.' Lord Howe looked furious at the libel on his party, but thoughtful too, especially when Tom Garth added, 'And you see the beauty of it, don't you?'

We both pondered for a moment.

'His late Majesty King George IV contracted an illegal marriage with Mrs FitzHerbert,' I said slowly, at last, 'but there were no children. The late Duke of York contracted no illegal marriage, and had no children of any kind. If the Duke of Clarence and Mrs Jordan *had* married, and if the marriage had been legitimised by Parliament, the FitzClarences would be the eldest grandchildren of George III, and the undoubted heirs to the throne. They would be the new royal family.'

'Precisely!' said Tom Garth. 'That's how George FitzClarence saw it.'

'But the whole thing, the whole elaborate fraud, depended on the life – or the death – of the Princess Victoria,' I said, with a severity I sincerely felt.

'What whole thing?' he asked, with pretended innocence.

'The supposed movement to get the FitzClarences legitimised. It would never happen while the Princess Victoria was alive.'

He shrugged.

'Probably not. Frankly it was never going to happen if she did die, but we managed to convince George otherwise. Anyway, you should ask him about that. I only supplied him with documents.'

'No, no, you can't get away with that,' said Lord Howe, standing over him sternly. 'You knew where the documents might lead.'

He was still absurdly cocky.

'Where the documents might lead was no responsibility of mine.'

'It most certainly was. And I'm sure you are aware that it has already led to an attempt on the life of the Princess.'

His jaw dropped open.

'Is that what you think?'

'It is.'

'Oh dear, I think you've really got hold of the wrong end of the stick there.'

I decided I had to step in.

'A death took place at the castle on the Princess's first day there,' I said.

He shrugged.

'Deaths do, don't they? I got a whiff of something up from overhearing footmen talk, and I've been nosing around a bit here and in London. I don't see there's any evidence for an attempt on the life of the Princess.'

168

'While the Duke of Cumberland was shooting in the air on the terraces poison was put in one of the glasses of the guests. Popper went round while everyone was crowded round the windows and drank down the unfinished glasses.'

Tom Garth thought for a moment, then leaned forward in his chair.

'And was the Princess's a wine glass?'

'Yes. The King had just pressed a glass of claret on her.'

'And was there the slightest possibility of her drinking the glass down?'

I was dumbfounded. The thought hadn't occurred to me.

'Well no, but . . . he couldn't know that . . .'

'Of course he could know that. What little girl of eleven downs a whole glass of claret? She sips it – if that – and puts it quickly aside.'

'But—'

'Another thing: on Friday, when the Princess came to the castle, George FitzClarence hadn't even got his hands on the supposed marriage certificate. He wouldn't have attempted the life of the Princess before he'd got that.'

'Are you suggesting that someone else attempted to kill her?' asked Lord Howe.

'No, I'm not. I'm suggesting that no one did.'

'And the man who died?'

There was a moment's silence in the room.

'Funny chap, George FitzClarence,' said Tom Garth, meditatively, or with a show of it. 'So fiery and precipitate in some ways, but with an odd vein of caution that makes him hold back.'

'He talked to me about not taking any steps that hadn't been thought out beforehand,' I admitted.

'He talked to me about making no moves with regard to the Princess before the ground had been well and truly prepared,' said Tom Garth, with a casualness that chilled the blood. 'He also talked about people who could be dispensed with, people no one would miss, no one would bother with.' He shot a sharply satirical eye in my direction. 'I think he was thinking of old people, people of no constitutional importance – *theatrical* people, for example, Mr Mozart. I'd say you had a lucky escape!'

I could hardly take it in.

'You mean Popper was the intended victim the whole time? That the poison was put in his glass?' I remembered something else that FitzClarence had said. 'That this was a sort of *rehearsal* for the real attempt?'

'That's what I'd guess. I put it down to his mother – that's where he got the instinct from: to try things out in advance. He wanted to prepare the ground, make sure he could get away with sending someone to a better world without too many questions being asked. You all obliged by hushing up the matter entirely At the theatre they don't seem to know where he died, let alone how. Of course the same would probably not have happened when he came to "take steps" about the Princess Victoria. But he was preparing the ground for an attempt on her that would leave him entirely in the clear.'

'Monstrous!' said Lord Howe. 'I can hardly believe it, even of him.'

I suspect he was thinking of the projected attempt on the Princess's life, rather than the actual murder of a theatre manager. Poor Mr Popper! To be thought of as one so insignificant as to be totally expendable. But Tom Garth was quite right: the most appalling thought was that it could have been ME. Possibly I was only protected by the fact that the King was showing me conspicuous favour.

I pondered, trying to avoid Lord Howe's eye, because I thought he was wanting to leave. But there were surely things, important things, to be sorted out first. The sense Tom Garth's explanation made was mad sense, but it was sense of a kind: the sort that a madman's brain might conceive. But George FitzClarence did not conceive this hideous plan in the madness of his jealous grievances. He was the tool, the man who did the things conceived in the brains of others. And this grubby scoundrel before us was only another tool. He could not have set these events in motion merely to gain a few pounds for forged documents. If George FitzClarence was the Othello, this man was the Rodrigo. Somewhere there was an Iago. Thinking upon the sequence of events, the happenings on the fatal day, the person who stood to gain, I thought there could be only one answer as to who that Iago was. I looked at Tom Garth.

'Up and down,' I said.

'What's that?' said Garth, frowning.

'You said in the Fox and Newt you needed contacts up and down, and you said you would never be the initiator, never the one who sets things in motion.' I stood up and looked down at him. 'Who was your contact *up*? Who was the person who put you up to this, paid you to make contact with George FitzClarence, fed his obsession, drove him to murder?'

'Now that,' said Tom Garth, 'is not in the contract.'

'It most certainly *is*,' said Lord Howe, now alert to what had to be done. 'We have to know the *whole* truth, or the contract is void, and you will have talked for no reward.'

Garth's eyes went here and there, but I sensed there was an amused glint in them, as if he was playing with us.

'He's a dangerous cove. Not to be crossed,' he said.

'The danger will be . . . neutralised,' Lord Howe promised. 'There must be no danger to the Princess, and there will be none to you. You, in any case, will be far away.'

'Not far enough,' grumbled Tom Garth. But then I saw the glint again. 'But I suppose for ten thousand I'll have to tell you. In fact it really is the cream of the jest.'

'The *jest*!' exploded Lord Howe.

'Yes – damned funny when you think about it.'

'*Funny*!'

'In the circumstances. Ironic I think they call it. In view of that letter we made up from the Duke of Wellington.'

Lord Howe still had not got it.

'Come on, man! I am not a man to be played with. Who was the instigator of this treasonable plot?'

Tom Garth leaned back in his chair and laughed loud and long. Finally he recovered his breath and faced us both.

'The instigator of this treason? Someone I should think you know very well, My Lord. It was the Duke of Cumberland. My father.'

171

EIGHTEEN
Finale

I did not talk to the King again until some ten days later. He was occupied with politicians on the evening of our interview with Tom Garth, and thinking he was unlikely to be in a good mood afterwards I withdrew from the castle, back to London and the humble peace of my rooms in Henrietta Street where, to tell you the truth, I felt much happier. It was a week later, when I was busy on a new commission, that I had a stiff little letter from Lord Howe telling me that the King would be at Buckingham Palace on the following Thursday and was anxious to talk to me.

I was not very anxious to talk to him. How was I to tell him part but not the whole truth about the affair which he had entrusted to me? For I was determined to shield his son, for his father's sake – for the King's, that is, and perhaps also a little for the man to whom he bore so close a resemblance, my dear old friend da Ponte, librettist extraordinary, philanderer supreme.

Was he in fact his son? Who can tell our paternities – life's greatest mystery? I can only say that in the early months of his stay in England dear Lorenzo was obsessed with the beauty and charm of Mrs Jordan, and those were the months in which George FitzClarence must have been conceived. No, I was determined: George FitzClarence I would leave to Lord Howe, who could be relied upon to deliver a warning as stern and cold as warning could be, along with a catalogue of what we knew about his misdeeds. Royalty are different from us: they are not accountable for their misdeeds. George FitzClarence was royalty, at least for the moment, because he was beloved of the King (as I am beloved of God in my name, and in my genius!).

So I went to my interview with the King apprehensive because

I did not know how far I would be able to skirt around the truth. As it turned out the King had other things on his mind. It was his first visit to what we must learn to call Buckingham Palace, and his dislike of the place when it was Buckingham House had intensified to loathing since his brother's extravagant refurbishment of it to make the Sovereign's London home.

'What does it look like, eh?' he demanded of me the moment I was shown into the Presence. 'A high-class whore-house, that's what it reminds me of.'

'I defer to Your Majesty's experience of such places,' I said daringly. The King let out a little bark of laughter, his pineapple head bobbing. 'It's difficult for me to imagine a brothel with so much gilt and plush. It puts me in mind of a very grand hotel – too grand for anyone to feel comfortable staying in.'

'That's what I shall treat it as,' said the King, looking around him with contempt. 'Stay the night and then leave. Maybe I can turn it into a barracks for the Foot Guards – they need a new one urgently. Or give it to the government for a new Houses of Parliament. But *what* a place, eh? What a *nasty* place. People don't want to live in all this sort of show-off finery, not these days. I tell you, I was happier at Bushey than I'll ever be in any of my palaces ...' A faraway look came into his eye, then the suspicion of a tear. But after a moment he pulled himself together. 'Ah well – what's past is past. Best get down to business, eh, Mr Mozart? What have you got to report?'

He gestured to one of the gilded chairs that so disgusted him, and it received me in a fat embrace. I cleared my throat, collected my thoughts, and began very tentatively.

'We have, I believe, got to the bottom of this business of Mr Popper's death.'

'Mr who?'

'Mr Popper, the theatrical manager.'

The King scratched his pineapple head.

'Oh yes, of course. I remember. I just think of it as the attempt on m'poor niece's life.'

'Naturally, Your Majesty. I'm afraid I have to tell you that the instigating force behind the whole scheme was your brother, the Duke of Cumberland.'

The veins in his forehead swelled alarmingly.

'Ernest! M'brother Ernest! I believe you. I would believe anything of that man. He's mad. What was it they said of that poet chappie? "Mad, bad, and dangerous to know"? That's m'brother Ernest to a tee.' He calmed down a little and sat there, thoughtful. At length he said, 'What do we do, eh? Eh?'

'There is no evidence against him that would stand up in a court of law.'

'Pity. They'd have had to hang him with a silken rope. I'd've enjoyed that. Shouldn't think it'd make it any nicer, would you?' He was getting warm again and took out his handkerchief. 'Still, frightful scandal, eh? Don't know that we could have survived one as bad as that. But he'll have to be kept away from little Victoria, eh?'

I nodded vigorously.

'Certainly, sir. It seems to me that the best thing would be for you to order him abroad for the duration of your reign. He will in any event become the King of Hanover on your death, if he outlives you.'

'Glad you added that. I'll do my best to see he doesn't. I can order him abroad, of course. But would he go? Never does anything anybody wants him to do.' He was puzzled, and rambled off the point. 'You know, they quite *like* him in Germany. Isn't that extraordinary. They know the type. What a vicious *clown* he is. That performance on the terraces! ... I suppose that was some kind of blind, a distraction?'

'Yes, Your Majesty. Of course there was no question of the Duke being directly implicated himself.'

'Of course there wasn't. Too damned cunning. Gets other people to do his dirty work for him.'

'Lord Howe has ensured that one of his agents, the man Tom Garth—'

The King looked comically penitent. I think he was used to that.

'Oh dear – Garth! Too kind there, was I? Misplaced charity?'

'I'm afraid so, sir. Lord Howe has paid him money to leave the country. Otherwise he certainly would have implicated Your Majesty's family.'

'Damned scoundrel!' said the King, missing the ambiguity

in my words. I felt I should pass on some information I had received by post that morning.

'Unfortunately Lord Howe in the written agreement specified that he should leave England.'

'What's wrong with that?'

'I heard this morning that he has in fact gone to Scotland. My correspondent – a fine musician in Edinburgh – tells me that he is in the city, is spending money lavishly and making great play with his . . . connection with the royal family. Some are shocked, but others are thrilled and receive him with open arms, even good families, I'm afraid.'

'That's the Scots,' said the King. 'Mad about royalty, even though they mistreated their own when they had them. The scoundrel! To talk about his mother . . . Ah well. That's the world, the modern world . . . So that's that then?'

I got up. No one was ever gladder at the end of an audience.

'Yes, that's that, sir.' I paused. 'About the Princess – I fear Your Majesties are not likely to see much of the little girl. I know how much you and the Queen would like to. But the Duchess is intensely jealous.'

'Pity, pity.'

'I wonder if you could put someone in the household, sir – someone young, who could both supply you with information, and perhaps be something of a playmate for the little girl. She very much needs one. There was a young footman at Windsor Castle who helped us greatly with Tom Garth. He would fit the bill excellently.'

'Capital idea! I'll put Lord Howe on to it. What about the mother and that scoundrel Conroy?'

'A *tendresse*, I suspect—'

'A what?'

'A sentimental affection, Your Majesty, but I do not believe there is a criminal connection.'

'Hmmm. Pity. Pity in a way. It would have made it easier to get rid of him.' He rummaged in his pocket, my eyes on him (I fear) greedily, and he finally came up with a promising-looking bag that clinked. 'Mr Mozart, I am grateful to you. Indebted too. The Queen and I will hope to see you again at Windsor.

175

Hear you play some of your pieces.' I took the bag, bowed, and began the process of bowing myself out. He stopped me with a roar as I was half-way out. 'I say, Mr Mozart, when I'm gone, what a *time* the nation will have when she's Queen! Reconciles one to popping off, eh? *Walk* out like a man, Mr Mozart – don't bother with all that nonsense.'

So I turned and walked out. But at the door I paused and looked back. The King had resumed his disgusted tour of the Palace, but the expression on his face was a happy one too. I wondered to what extent the interview had gone well because the King *wanted* to keep some things hidden – at some deep level of his mind he was hardly conscious of, where suspicions of his son probably lurked. I had a sudden vision of the years that remained for him: all the disappointments and disillusions that lay ahead, all the family crises and quarrels, all the unreasonable demands, all the political storms he would have to weather, all the personal quagmires he would have to skirt. I felt so sorry for the poor old booby, whom I'd really come to like, that I felt glad I had not given him, at the beginning of his reign, what would have been the greatest disillusion of all: the truth about his son.

As luck would have it that afternoon was to see my first lesson with the Princess since her visit to the castle. I dined at a chop-house in Kensington, and, thinking we would probably not be able to talk, scribbled one of those little notes for her that I knew she would enjoy receiving.

M.D.
The King was enchanted by the success of your visit to Windsor, which was a popular triumph. Do nothing about the matter we talked of. Knowledge unused is future power.

Your friend.

I thought she would like that last apophthegm – would ponder its wisdom before going to sleep at night. I finished my wine and walked to the palace. The scruffy footman, Ned Dorkle, actually seemed pleased to see me.

''Ear you've 'ad exciting times up at ʋne castle,' he said,

winking. 'Maybe we should 'ave a drink and you can tell me all about them.'

'And have them passed on to the illustrated magazines of Paris?' I said, with mock horror. 'A confidential royal servant has to be able to keep secrets better than that.'

He smirked. It was interesting, I thought, that there was a servant network that apparently kept royal secrets perpetually in circulation.

The Princess, who was brought into the music room by Lehzen, was much too circumspect to bubble on about her Windsor visit, or give any indication that she was intoxicated by the splendour of the social set she had mingled with there. She gave me her little hand as usual, and then sat down demurely, saying, 'Now I am *really* going to have to play better if people are to be forced to listen to me play in public.' Before she launched into her first piece of Clementi fiddle-faddle I was able to slip her my note, which she tucked into her dress. She played moderately well, confirming my view that there was real musicality there. However, at the end of the piece Lehzen got up.

'I hev a great deal to prepare for the Princess's history lesson today. I vill deny myself the pleasure of listening to the rest of the music lesson.'

'Heaven!' said the Princess, as soon as the door closed. 'Now we can talk about those wonderful days at Windsor, which I shall remember for the rest of my life. Are not the King and Queen the most delightful old people?'

I smiled.

'They are indeed like a breath of fresh air. But the Queen is hardly an old person – she is younger than your Mama.'

'Well, is not Mama an old person?' A look of steel came into her expression, something I had noticed occasionally before. 'Unfortunately age is no guarantee of good conduct.'

'My dear—'

'But let's not talk about that *yet*. You must tell me, dear Mr Mozart, what was *going on*.'

'Going on, my dear?'

'Yes, going on. Something was: after all your queries and commands of me you can hardly deny that. Something between you and the King and that awful, slimy Lord Howe. Oh, I shan't have to have anything to do with *him* when I become Queen, shall I? And what were you having that conference with Mrs Hattersley about? It was so frustrating not to be able to hear a single word! Now, tell me what it was. Did it have anything to do with Sir John Conroy?'

'Er . . . not directly. Though there was some discussion about Sir John. In confidence I can say that the King, to use his kind of language, doesn't like the cut of his jib.'

She frowned.

'Is that naval? What does it mean?'

'I have no idea, my dear. But in ordinary language it means that he is the sort of person that most people feel is not to be trusted.'

'Very true. How *wise* of the dear old King! And how unlike *some other people*. But if it wasn't about Sir John, who was it about?'

'My dear, I am sworn to secrecy, and couldn't possibly tell you. Suffice it to say that there was some . . . some little intrigue concerning yourself which we have nipped in the bud.'

She puffed up her chubby cheeks in outrage.

'I should think so! I will not have people intriguing about me without my knowledge.' She played on for a bit and then said, shooting a sidelong glance at me out of her little piggy eyes, 'George FitzClarence is the most handsome man I have ever seen in my life.'

My face was a mask.

'He is very good-looking.'

'But is he as *good* as he is handsome?'

'He gets his looks from his mother, who was a most handsome and charming lady. I would also say, in her way, *good*. Let us hope that he has inherited that too.'

'Well, he certainly doesn't get his looks from his father, does he?' she said, giggling. 'But I'm sure the King is in his way good too, so he is lucky to have such a father and mother. But I'm sure speaking of the FitzClarences' mother would not be approved of. I think you only mentioned her to change the subject, Mr Mozart.'

'I wasn't aware of changing the subject. I knew Mrs Jordan much better than I know George FitzClarence.'

'And you are not on any account going to tell me what was going on at Windsor?'

'I *can't*, my dear. Loyalty to the King prevents me. When you are Queen you will want to be able to call on such loyalty.'

She played on, thoughtfully.

'Hmmm. I suppose so. I shall be *jolly* nasty to anyone who doesn't show it! . . . Oh, I haven't read your note.' She executed some slapdash left-hand scales as she retrieved the note from the bosom of her dress and read it, smiling and then serious. 'I'm glad the dear King was pleased. "Unused knowledge is future power." How very true, Mr Mozart. I shall think about that often. But Mr Mozart – it may be that I shall have to use it *soon*.'

'No, no, my dear, that would be most unwise. It will then be quite useless.'

'But I may *have* to. There is something up, Mr Mozart – something about *you*. I'm awfully afraid they are going to rob me of the *great pleasure* of having lessons from you.'

This was a blow.

'Why would they do that?'

'I don't know. I think it is because they know you are a friend, and they don't like that. I'm not to have friends. But nobody could replace you, Mr Mozart – not even the lovely Mr Mendelssohn.' She looked at me with a sparkle in her eyes, teasing me. 'It's true – he could not be so jolly and funny and wise – to be wise you have to be old. And I'm sure you would be inconsolable too.'

'I should be very sad.'

'It would leave a gap in your life which it would be impossible to fill,' she insisted, only half in joke. 'You would have nothing left to live for.'

I smiled at her.

'My dear, I am a composer. I have music to live for. Recently I have been much more active than I have been for years. Music is flowing out of me. Only the other day an odd-looking man came to my apartment and commissioned me to write a requiem. I am setting about the commission with a great deal of pleasure.'

She shivered.

'A requiem! I can't see how you can be so pleased at writing that kind of music. You're not going to go all gloomy on me, are you, Mr Mozart?'

'No, my dear. The music I write has no effect on my everyday face. I'm just telling you that I have other things in my life beside my lessons with you.'

'I suppose it's just as well,' she admitted, launching into the early sonata of mine that she had been practising. 'Because you can't get much *musical* pleasure from them, I suppose.'

'I get a great deal of *human* pleasure from them,' I said truthfully. 'And I shall do my best to make sure I go on doing so.'

'Oh, *please* do, Mr Mozart.'

'Do nothing yourself. Leave it all to me.'

'I would *love* to see Sir John worsted.'

'I shall do my best, my dear.'

At that moment Ned Dorkle put his head round the door, his wig comically askew as usual.

'Time for the Princess's 'istory lesson.' He added, as the Princess, smiling happily, scurried off, 'And it's you for Sir John, Mr Mozart.'

He said it with an ominous tone. As we walked sedately down the corridor, he added, 'Something's up. Lehzen was closeted wiv 'is nibs for ten minutes after she came out from the music lesson. Watch for yourself, Mr Mozart.'

'I shall, my friend,' I said serenely.

Sir John was standing behind his desk when I was ushered into his little counting-house of an office – sleek, plump, pleased with himself, unwise. I had begun to dislike him. I felt like a soldier girding up his loins for battle (not that I really understand how one does gird up one's loins).

'Ah, Mr Mozart. The lesson has gone well?'

The polite preliminaries. I would play the game along with him.

'Very well, Sir John. The Princess is making great strides. The King was of course over-kind in asking her to play in public, but she is certainly improving.'

'Good, good . . . And I'm sure she will continue to improve with another teacher.'

180

I feigned surprise.

'I beg your pardon, Sir John?'

He looked down at me, a cat-like smile on his face.

'I think you heard me, Mr Mozart. We have decided that this will be your last lesson with the Princess.'

'And may I ask why that decision has been taken?'

He waited for a moment, to relish his words.

'Too many notes, Mr Mozart. Too many whispered conversations, too much giggling and sharing jokes. I'm afraid the Duchess and I are adamant that nobody, not even someone as old as yourself, could possibly be on such terms with the heiress to the throne.'

The Princess was right, then. They were trying to keep her from all friendships, from anyone who would love her. One day she would love, and it would not be her mother, not Sir John, not Lehzen. It would be a great love – the greater because of the arid desert of the emotions which they had tried to create around her.

'You are making a great mistake, you know,' I said.

He swelled like a turkey-cock and, oozing pomposity, took out his watch and looked at it ostentatiously.

'I hardly think, whatever favour you may currently enjoy at court, that it is your business to lecture me – or the Duchess, through me – on the upbringing of the Heiress Presumptive.'

I ignored him.

'A child has strong affections. If they can find no other outlet they may turn into equally strong aversions. This is true of the Princess – especially true. And it could have terrible consequences for you and her mother when she comes to the throne. You would lose every ounce of influence you otherwise might have had.'

'My time is valuable, Mr Mozart. Please take your fee. This terminates the Princess's connection with you.'

'I think not,' I said, not stirring or taking the proffered money.

'Most assuredly it does.'

Reluctantly I played my last card. Better I played it than the Princess used it against her mother.

'Unfortunately for you, Sir John, the Princess strayed into

the woods during the picnic in Windsor Great Park.' A shadow crossed his eyes. 'She saw there something that shocked her very much. I had difficulty dissuading her from going to the King about it. Now you and I, Sir John, are men of the world.' (I blasphemed against my genius. I am a man of the universe!) 'We know that what she saw was – how shall I put it? – a display of harmless affection. But the Princess has been insulated from the world and its ways, and her judgements are extreme and immature. It will be very bad from every point of view if she brings this matter out into the open with her mother.'

'She wouldn't dare,' he blustered.

'You little know her. She certainly would, and already wants to. If she does the servants will get to know, and the information will be hawked to the more scandalous newspapers here, to the illustrated magazines on the Continent. Matters would be still worse if she went to the King.'

'She would not be *allowed* to go to the King.'

'She would not have to go in person. She could use an emissary. Someone the King trusted.' I looked at him long and hard. 'That emissary would be willing to go if he thought it in the Princess's best interests.'

His soldier's body was rigid with fury.

'It is intolerable to be subjected to blackmail!'

'I'm sure it is. The sensible course is to give no grounds for blackmail in the first place.'

There was a long pause. Finally he said, 'Very well. The lessons continue.'

There were a lot of pieces of advice I could have given him, particularly about the conduct of the household's financial affairs. But what right had I, of all people, to give advice on money matters? I thought, in any case, he was unlikely to be in receptive mood.

'Thank you, Sir John. I'm sure that your decision will be as satisfactory to the Princess as it is to me.'

As I bowed I caught sight of his face. He was fuming. I thought it wisest to leave the room at once. I did so with a spring in my step. I had attained my aim. The lessons would continue for as long as I could hold the threat over him. My high-spirits were augmented as I walked down the corridor at hearing the Princess's charming voice. The door to the room where she was having her history lesson was open, due to the warmth of the day. Lehzen, her back to me, was pointing out something on a chart – no, it was a family tree. As she prepared to study it, the Princess saw me lingering in the corridor.

'Dair is His present Majesty,' Lehzen said, pointing with a pencil, 'and dair is Your Royal Highness.'

The Princess appeared to study it for some time, then looked up. In her clear, bell-like voice, clearly enunciating for posterity she said, 'I will be good.'

And as Lehzen bent over her notebook to record the words, the Princess looked at me over her governess's shoulder and winked.